Certain Dawn,
Inevitable Dawn

stories

Tasha Haas

December 2010

Editor: Kevin Rabas

Woodley Press
Department of English
Washburn University
1700 SW College Avenue
Topeka, Kansas 66621

Printed by Lightning Source

ISBN: 978-0-9828752-1-6
Library of Congress Control Number: 2010942671

Cover art: Krista Heller

Cover design: Kevin Rabas, Tom Besgrove, Tasha Haas and
Pam LeRow

Author photo: Kevin Rabas

Text design and layout: Pam LeRow

To contact the author, write to:
Tasha Haas
757 Washington Road
Lawrence, KS 66044
thaas@kckcc.edu

Acknowledgements

The author gratefully acknowledges the following publications, in which versions of these stories first appeared:

"A Familiar White Corridor," *South Dakota Review*, Winter 1999/2000

"nightgown," *South Dakota Review*, Winter 2003/2004

"Nurse Drops Baby, Runs," published as "All There Is" in *Stickman Review*, December 2007

"Spring, Sunday Morning," *Coal City Review*, January 2005

"The Woman in the Wings," *Kansas City Kansas Community College E-Journal*, October 2009

Words of Thanks

Thank you to my editor, Kevin Rabas, and to Dennis Etzel, Jr. for wanting to publish this manuscript. My gratitude and regard to Woodley Press for its committed support of regional authors.

Thank yous to Kansas City Kansas Community College, The Julia and David White Artists' Colony, and the Lawrence Arts Center for the Langston Hughes Award for "Spring, Sunday Morning," a recognition which, in many ways, jump-started this collection coming together.

Thank you to Krista Heller for the flower sculptures, and Tom Besgrove for help on the cover. Thank you to Pam Le-Row for the prompt and excellent layout and design work.

An especially warm thank you to Kevin Rabas and Wendell Mayo for their encouragement and suggestions on many of these stories, and their faith in my writing over the years. Thanks for being my best readers—as well as writers to emulate, writers blazing your own paths.

Thank you to my family for always being there and always caring.

Finally, I thank the creative spirit that flows in everyone for giving me these mysterious characters and their mysterious tales.

Tasha Haas
December 2010

Introduction

Tasha Haas's debut collection of short stories asserts her as a strong, tough-minded writer who also has a deft, subtle touch, and it is obvious in this collection that she loves and admires her lead characters and respects her darker, malevolent characters, in turn. This is the sign of a balanced, wise intelligence. Furthermore, her stories have a lyricism, an attention to each word, that is beautiful and admirable, marking her as a craftsman of the language. Hers is a new voice, but one that might one day rank alongside the stylistic voices of Virgina Woolf, Henry James, Joan Didion, Don DeLillo, and Aimee Bender. Haas's is a meditative, lyrical style, philosophical but concrete, searching, yet driven and focused. At times, she meanders and improvises, but in the way jazz master John Coltrane moves with grace, skill, and acuity through a long, long set of solo choruses. For instance, in "nightgown" Haas explores the image and symbol of this cover, this sleepwear that holds her main character in so many ways that the nightgown almost has life and is a spirit that tugs the narrator along and out into the cornfields and night: "The back of the gown hugs her calves and fishtails out front between them. Like this it begins to move, and she feels its force, not the force of the wind but the force of the nightgown. Or the spirit in the nightgown." It is this sharpness to detail, this skill with image and symbol, that makes Haas's stories sing and burn into memory. Her world is vivid and meaningful. It is not a world of dead things, but instead a world full of life and fire, a world her characters spend their lives interpreting. They engage with corn and the night and the thin fingernail paring moon. Her characters stumble into trouble and grapple with it. In "Spring, Sunday Morning," a former priest relocates to start a new life, and an unknown, apparently motiveless visitor kills him. In "Nurse Drops Baby, Runs," a baby slips from a nurse's hands in the hospital, and she flees, abandoning her car, her job, her old life. She goes on the run. This collection is inhabited by strong, autonomous women characters, characters that are up to the problems they face. They grow stronger in the heat of adversity, and they spar with the men around them, and often win. Haas's work here is intoxicating, and even when her stories appear like brutal, fiery wrecks along the road, we cannot keep from slowing down and looking. What we see might be shocking and might be grisly, but we can only hope we engage with that scene before us with understanding and love and grace, and really look and see, and have that kind of vision Haas does.

Kevin Rabas
November 2010

Spring, Sunday Morning

Spring, Sunday morning, and a friend has just called with terrible news: her childhood priest murdered, left to die alone on the floor of his new apartment a week or longer, a startling testament this lovely morning, prisms of light and shadow revolving in the treetops, silver leaves clattering in the wind, sheer blue sky, Sunday morning, day of reverence, day to recognize the sanctity of all of this, all, all, Sunday morning, spring, then the phone call, terrible news, news of the cold heartedness of God, of His sick sense of humor, what we feared most shown true. Left to die alone a death that may have lasted an hour, may have lasted a week, and the thought of him, whom I never knew, lying in that city apartment, an apartment that had been lived in and lived in and lived in but in which he would not live long, the thought makes me wonder who he was and who He is, these two Fathers at once, the Father who was and the Father who is, as it must have made him wonder, sent him from this life wondering, who was this God who had destined such a death for him? Was it this God who knocked? It was predicted he would knock—behold, I stand at the door and knock—behold, behold. All his life had been a straining to behold. Now he heard a knock. Late in the evening, Holy Thursday, he'd just returned from what to him was the most beautiful of masses, he sat in a pew toward the back remembering when it had been he who washed the feet as Jesus washed the feet of his disciples at the Last Supper, showing that divine love expressed itself not in being served but in serving. As the priest—his replacement—moved down the aisle washing the feet of the fold, ordinary, human feet, as he watched he remembered cradling the foot in the white cloth, dipping his fingers in the chalice to catch holy water and sending it in droplets onto the foot. But he was no longer a priest, he was an ex-priest, starting over in the middle of his life in a new city and for this reason he could not imagine who was knocking, for he knew few people yet in the city that crawled and pulsed and throbbed all hours of the day and night, most days as he traversed the concrete he felt husklike, a skin of garlic, transparent and drifting in his lay clothes, insubstantial khakis and a white button-down. He was not used to the anonymity of the city, of course. He had grown up and spent the first twenty years of his priesthood, the second twenty years of his life, in a small rural city in Iowa, where eventually everyone knew him, where he became someone, always, with dimension, the full bulb and weight and swell of personhood about him. He was known, and he enjoyed this fullness for so long, he did not resist it, in fact he never resisted it, but in the end it resisted him, for underneath in him, things had started moving, shifting, spreading, and these pressed against the borders by which he was known, which were, perhaps, the only ways one could be known. That was how it was with God, for instance, we could never know the totality of God—Enoch walked with God and was not—only by His outlines did we know Him, His manifestations in the world. Similarly he was known by his fold, known and known until there was no one else he could be—he was Father Bren (Irish), forty-four, entered the priesthood at twenty, youngish yet, studious as a priest should be, always reading, drove the white Audi, family in Cedar Rapids. He was *their* Father Bren. His sheep became his possessors, he the shepherd their possessed. Then, suddenly, it seemed, he no longer knew the Father they knew, he didn't know who they were speaking to when they spoke to him, he had different answers when they came to him in confession or private counsel about their faithlessness, their betrayals, their doubts, their confusion, their lack of awe—their deficiencies, more often what they had discovered missing in themselves than what was there, and he began to suspect this was part of the problem, maybe all of it, and he told them this, suggested it, that is, and no, they didn't like it. He suggested—and it seemed to come from outside himself, this counsel, he really wasn't sure where it came from, but he hoped it was God—he suggested they look at what they were and not at what they thought they should be, start from there no matter how dark and awful that was, it was not what a priest should say—a priest said, resist! resist! never, accept, open. He opened, then, to his next life, and left, just like that, Iowa to Chicago, knowing the lightness of no robes, and found the apartment, and moved in and began to live there and that was how he came to be sitting under the tall copper lamp with his book when the knock came—behold—when the knock came, he opened, but not before he had opened the door to the new apartment and found it so, so empty, as of course it should have been, but he had not expected it, so much emptiness, and it struck him that this was the emptiness that lay beyond the shelter of the priesthood, the emptiness of the layman's life, a life made alone in an unbordered wilderness absent of doctrine, absent of heaven, absent of hell and absent of, well, furniture. The apartment was dingy, white walls, nappy beige carpet, squared white tile, tile he would spend his last hours, or days, staring at inches from his face, tile he would get to know well. The apartment was not cheap or slummish, it was an average city apartment, it was just the used quality of it, the lived in and lived in and abandoned of it that startled him at first. But he moved his things in, and they were nice things, a middle-aged priest's things, for that was who he was, a middle-aged ex-priest, youngish yet, he hung the icons from Madagorje and the crucifix from Macedonia and the rosaries from Jerusalem and the place improved rapidly, and began to resemble a home, which was how he came to be sitting there in the recliner, his feet unslippered and unwashed—he had been sitting in the middle of the pew—in the joint shelter of the Macedonian crucifix and the cone of light from the tall copper lamp, reading, near to bed, Merton again, who had served his whole life a monk and now the church wouldn't sell him in their bookstores, a punishment for the work he did at the end of his life, work he'd died doing in fact, electrocuted by the loose wire of a ceiling fan in a cheap hotel room in Thailand, work to bring together Buddhism and Christianity, or at least to start talking to them, the others. He was reading Merton when the knock came at the door, Merton on hope, no man is an island—hope lies in this, that no man is an island—when he heard the knock at the door, a knock of normal force, nothing unusual about it, or had it been particularly soft, the knocker conscientious of the late hour? It was about eleven, he didn't know many people in the city yet, he couldn't imagine who it was, knocking at this hour without having called first. He went to the door. He looked through the peephole. The chain was fastened above three deadbolts, the door steel. The apartment was near the Catholic college he was working to raise funds for, not the worst neighborhood, not the best either, the kids lingered on the corners and he hated to think what was in their bulging pockets, drugs or guns or both. They were the reason the college was there, of course, and one reason he was there, but he wasn't good at stopping to talk to them, not yet. He should have been, he thought—how long he had been a priest—but the kids in this city looked differently than the ones in his own, even if they shared the tattoos, torn black tee-shirts, chains, piercings, and tight, small eyes. He would pass by without so much as looking at them even though he felt their eyes on him all the while. He was no longer a priest and no longer wore the authority of his black robes, the immunity of his robes, an immunity he had hidden in all his adult life, now, he was alone—when he looked through the peephole, and saw how dark it was in the hall, suddenly he felt alone. Why wasn't the hall light on? It was so dark he could make out no one through that hole, not even a shape. Yet the knocking came again. He could speak, but once he did, he would be thrown into new territory, his presence revealed. He hesitated. A quick prayer, for guidance. During the prayer the knocker spoke. It's the landlord, he said, a typical male voice, no accent that he could tell. It's the landlord, the voice said again. Open up. It could be. He'd never met the landlord, it had all been done by phone. The knocks came again, firmer, insistent. Open up. Father Bren slid the chain along its track and brought it loose. He started at the bottom with the deadbolts. He flipped the first, heard the heavy thunk of the iron cylinder retreating and the knocker must have heard it too, and the same sound on the second, and the third. Only the flimsy turn lock on the knob remained. He hesitated—Behold, I stand at the door and knock. He turned the final lock. If anyone hears my voice and opens the door—the seal broke, the door opened half an inch—I will enter his house—and slammed into him. He felt the force, the mighty anger behind the door, and fled. Not far. The club, hammer, bat, or bottle, hit him from behind, landing in the ridge at the base of the skull, the brainstem. On impact he felt a shocking tingling branch from his spine through his body, into the limbs, the fingers and toes, all in an instant, an instant followed by the deadly creep of numbness that would finally overtake his body. He fell forward, limbs helpless. There was the sickening snap of his neck, then the final slap of his cheek on the tile. It would not move again even though he lay conscious for hours, or days. A week passed before they found him. He had plenty of time to wonder who his God was. I wonder what conclusions he came to. It's spring, Sunday morning, prisms of light and shadow revolve in the treetops, leaves lift and turn carelessly, and the brutality of the world is close, it presses in, as close as the clattering of the wind in the leaves, as close as the Fathers, and their terrible stories.

Nurse Drops Baby, Runs

I heard the baby hit before I saw it. A soft thunk sound, muffled but solid. I looked and saw what had made that sound and it was the baby's head hitting the marble floor of the hospital. It didn't make a sound after that. Didn't squeal, didn't cry, but its mouth opened and closed, opened and closed but nothing came out. A second later that stopped too, and the baby was still.

It wasn't like it jumped out of my arms. I dropped it. That was the truth.

It was brand new. Its body red and hot and sticky still, its eyes slits with a tiny prick of light between the pink lids. She'd held it maybe five minutes, then I took it to clean it up. The father was there too, both of them smiling hard. I don't think the father held it.

I was going down the hall with it. I wasn't daydreaming that I remember, I wasn't thinking about anything special. I wasn't talking to it and not looking at it either. I had seen it as it came out and it was sweet and ugly, it was a miracle like they all are and it looked perfectly healthy. But I was working now, working the middle of the shift, when I didn't get sentimental during the births, I just didn't because there was plenty of work to do and I had to do it.

Thirteen years a nurse and I'd never done anything like this. I'd made mistakes, all of us did. Kept a woman in the sweat room all night after a C-section when she didn't need to be there. She came out hot and cranky, but alive. Maybe thirteen was my unlucky year.

It was heavy in my arms, a thick live weight through the blanket. Then my arms were light. I don't know.

It was late, around two. It was dark and quiet in the hall. I picked it up and held it to me and my hands were shaking. It wasn't moving and I was sure it was dead. I looked up and down the hall. Nobody. Rounded shapes of light lay on the floor at each door from the nightlights in the occupied rooms. One door showed no light and I remembered it was empty. I went into it. The room was dark except for a piece of blue streetlight across the bed next to the window. I laid it in that light and then I began to shake it as if I could shake the life back into it. I kept my eyes on its eyes, but the color was dull in the slits, there was no glimmer now and the eyes weren't seeing anything. I knew it was dead and I stopped and looked at it lying there dead on the clean tight sheet and then I went out, leaving it in the dark room, in the blue light on its dead face.

I walked down the hall to the stairwell. I took the stairs to the basement and walked down another hall and another, past Records and the locker rooms and I came out in the parking garage. I didn't meet anyone. As I crossed the empty garage I thought of my cigarettes and keys in my locker but I didn't stop.

Outside I crossed the big parking lot. Then there was the gravel lot then the wide sidewalk then the lake. I walked a long time along the lake's curve looking at the ships. They were small and white out on the water. Their sharp sides rose high off the water. They looked like paper boats in the darkness. They looked like you could push them over with your finger. Strings of windows lit up their sides. They were cargo ships but at first I thought they were cruise ships. I looked at them for a long time as I walked and thought about the people inside, the people dancing and drinking martinis. Living it up.

On the way back I kept my eyes on the stars. They were far up in the sky to the north over Lake Michigan and there were not many, but there were some. I didn't want to come to the hospital when it came but I put the feeling away and went straight in through the back to my locker. The lights were on bright on the bright green lockers but no one was in there. There were a few people I couldn't see because if I did, I would break. I couldn't see Doreen and I couldn't see Ray. I didn't see them. In the locker were scrubs and a couple changes of clothes and a pair of tennis shoes and a Stephen King novel. All of this I left. They could have it. I took the rain jacket I'd worn in that evening when the rain had been coming in gray slices and felt my keys and cigarettes in it and went out. Later I wished I'd taken the Stephen King.

As I drove home it was getting light. The light was all on the door when I unlocked it, that clear pale gray morning light. Usually when I came home it was still dark, usually about an hour away from light. Today was a different morning. I went in and the apartment too looked different. Smaller, and dim and cluttered even though it wasn't that cluttered. The apartment was nice. It had some nice things in it, things my ex and I had gotten together. The matching couches and the glass coffee table and the framed landscape prints of mountains that reminded Dennis of Colorado, where he grew up. The fresh daisies I'd bought at the grocery store the day before sat on the coffee table, the light through the blinds hitting some of them.

I went to the kitchen, dumped the old coffee filter and saw the trash needed taking out. I put a new filter in and two scoops of coffee. I stood looking at the coffee in the filter, I never did turn the coffeemaker on. I looked at my hands, then each finger and fingernail. The ragged hangnails. The red cracked skin from so much washing with antiseptic, no matter how much lotion I used.

I went into the bedroom and sat on the end of the bed. My thoughts ran in circles, from why to how to what kind of person was I that it had happened to me or I had let it happen, what kind of horrible person, but I knew the answer to that, it was murderer, that's what kind. Then to if only I could go back, go back, go back to that single moment or the moment just before that moment. The slightest tightening of my arms, that was all it would take to bring everything back. I saw the headline: "Nurse Drops Baby, Runs." I saw myself run. Run. Run. Run. Then the thoughts would start again, same circle.

An hour, two hours, I don't know. I was looking at the bedcover, the big violet flowers on it, and it was just like a hotel bedcover. It had been on my bed for years and I had liked it fine but I had never seen how it was exactly like a hotel bedcover, thin and nappy and gaudy in that way. Cheap and infested.

I went to the bathroom and changed from my scrubs into jeans and a tee-shirt, my hands dreamlike on my body. Not looking in the mirror I opened the medicine cabinet and took a tube of lipstick. It's funny how the only thing I took was lipstick, no toothbrush, no toothpaste, no moisturizer. I still wasn't thinking too clearly at that point. My purse I had left in the car, so when I went out that was the only thing I was holding—the lipstick clutched like a rock or a secret weapon in my fist.

In the car it was really light now. The light was all over inside the car. You could see how the air was all thick and glittery with dust. The air is always like that but you don't see it. You don't notice because you don't care, your mind is on other things, on your life and your petty problems.

I drove out south of Chicago and got on the interstate. The rest of that day and night I drove. The further out I got, the more stars there were in the windshield. I watched them like I had never watched anything before, like everything I was depended on that watching.

In Wichita it was morning again and I had to stop. There were truck stops and finally I went into one. I ordered coffee. I hadn't had any yet and I never go without my coffee.

Before she brought it I went into the bathroom. I went to the bathroom and washed my hands and dried them and looked around. At the dirty tile and the smudged striped wallpaper and the black and green grime lining the base of the sink where it met the tile and it occurred to me I hadn't done anything wrong. I ran my hands over my face and stroked my head, my tangled hair. My hair is thin and I could feel the shape of my head through it, long and oval, all bone. I stroked it a while. I cupped my hands over my face. I looked in the mirror through my fingers. Slowly I took my hands down. I didn't look good but there was the same basic shape of the face I had always had underneath, a face I hadn't minded. I felt in my purse for the lipstick and put it on. It was dark, plum, evening lipstick. I always liked that lipstick, I always felt good in it. I put it on heavy, too heavy. I smacked my lips and looked. They were dark and thick and I looked ready for something.

When I came out the coffee was there, and it was cold. The light on its surface tilted and shook, reflecting the light fixtures in the diner. The men were sitting around smoking and drinking coffee, some in circles around tables and some alone. They were not the kind of men I was used to. Dennis had sold computers at a discount warehouse. The doctors and residents and the other nurses were modest and clean-shaven and they didn't wear hats. Everything about these men was rough-edged, their faces and voices and the scrapes of their boots under the table as they grunted at each others' jokes. Their bellies in plaid western shirts hung over their belt buckles. Some wore cowboy hats, others greasy baseball caps with trucking company logos. I sat holding the coffee in its thick cup up close, breathing into it as if it were hot. Finally I paid and went out.

As I was going out a man came toward me down the narrow fake wood paneled hall. He wore jeans and a blue mesh baseball cap and a well-trimmed beard, brown with silver patches. As he passed I hesitated and turned toward him, I don't know why. He paused too, in his eyes a question like should-I-know-you, then he went on, into the lounge, a little room filled with smoke and a television with the volume on very low. A Mexican kid was sitting on the vinyl couch with his legs stretched out staring at the television. The man sat on the other couch. He looked up and saw me standing in the doorway. He looked back at the television. I went in.

There were the two couches, a recliner near the television and a metal folding chair at the end of the man's couch. I sat in this chair. The length of the couch was between us and we were facing the same way, not each other. I stared at the kid's pointed cowboy boots, thinking of the baby. A soap opera in Spanish was on.

Pretty soon I heard the man strike a match and light a cigarette. I felt him looking at me. With my plum lipstick on.

"Smoke?" he said. His eyes had deep creases around them and his brows were thick and gray under the hat but his beard was mostly brown and he had strong, symmetrical features. His eyes were oddly pale, though in that light I couldn't tell if they were blue or green.

"I have my own," I said, still looking at the kid's boots. I got my pack from my purse and lit one.

"Where you headed?" he said. I pulled on the cigarette and saw it was trembling.

He looked back at the television. I opened my mouth and closed it.

"Denver?" It came out as a question. My voice trembling too.

"Funny. Me too."

I stared at the tip of the cigarette. I felt him looking at me, felt him thinking.

After a long pause he said, "You looking for a ride?"

The kid looked over and I looked back. I raised my eyebrows at him, like what's-it-to-you. Without looking at the trucker I said, "Why not?"

For a few minutes he didn't say anything. Then he stood up. He came and touched my shoulder and I stood and we went out, his hand trailing down my back.

We crossed the big parking lot to his truck without speaking. It was a metallic blue truck with Schooner Trucking Co., Lincoln, Nebraska scrolled on the door. He stepped up on the high step and opened the door and stepped back down to let me climb in. I did and shut the door. On the console I saw his things: a miniature American flag, a tin of lip balm, cassette tapes, a wooden rosary hanging from the rearview. Maybe he wasn't a bad guy. It didn't matter. It was quiet, perfectly still in the cab. So still the cab shimmered. The morning was in it that same clear hard gray light it had been at home.

He got in beside me. I could smell his sweat and his deodorant over it. I stared through the big windshield. Men were crossing the lot, going to and from their trucks, and there were some cars parked in front of the restaurant and some getting gas. My car over there across the parking lot. He rubbed his face and yawned.

"Didn't stop last night," he said. I looked between the seats in the back. There was a sleeper, a blanket pulled tight over it and a pillow. It was dark and clean. I climbed back on it. I waited for his hand on me as I went but it didn't come.

I sat on the sleeper with my legs out in front of me. He was looking straight through the windshield. His hair was buzzed short, silver along the neckline. I saw the shave under the plastic strap of the hat, the clean brown back of his neck. I took my shirt off. I had a thick white bra on. I took that off, too.

Finally he turned, saw me, and looked back through the windshield. I rolled over on the sleeper and covered my head in my arms. I started to break. Then I felt his forearms on either side of me, close to my bare sides. He was climbing back, his weight on his arms. I felt my body stiffen.

When he was stretched out I turned over and put my hand on that clean back of neck. I pulled him to me.

"What do you think?" he said. His eyes were very pale green and serious. He wasn't bad-looking, he had a kind of Mel Gibson look.

"Nothing," I said. I pushed his hat off and ran my hand up his head, up the ridge where the two bones in the back meet. That was the spot it hit, that soft back of head on the marble floor. I pulled harder and kissed him and he kissed back. I felt the heavy lipstick smearing his lips.

I kissed him until he got hard. I tugged at his jeans and he unzipped them and pulled them down past his knees and I pulled mine down. His penis was cold and wet on the tip but it was hard. He pushed against me and it had been a long time. Maybe three years, since Dennis. Then he was inside me and it felt good. I had forgotten. The very first of him inside felt so good. Then it didn't anymore, it was rough and sad and the morning was coming in the cab gray and clear and hard.

He sat up and climbed half up front, his butt to me, balls swinging between his legs. He came back with a pack of cigarettes and dug a lighter out of his jeans. He sat with his back against the cab and I lay on my side with my head by his cold white hip. His penis fell toward my face, empty and wrinkled, gray-pink.

He handed me a cigarette and I took it. He lit it, then his own. I pulled in the smoke and let it out and he did the same. The sleeper filled with smoke, it moved into the front cab and mixed with the light. The rosary was hanging motionless in the light.

"Are you Catholic?" I said.

"Not really. Mom was."

"You don't believe in that stuff."

"Nah. I don't believe in nothing I can't see for myself. I never come across no evidence there's nothing else, d'you?"

"So all there is is what is."

"That's it. All there is is what is." He rubbed his hand on my bare belly. "I like the way you put it. That's a good way to put it."

He blew smoke out his nose and grinned down at me. He raised his eyebrows. His lips were plum color with my lipstick, it looked funny. Police, I thought. The law. That's what is.

"What's Denver like?" I said.

He shrugged. "Just another town. Mountains in back of it."

"You still offering that ride?"

"I never turn down company," he said. "Gets awful boring out there."

"Let's go."

He looked at me. "Don't you got a bag or something?"

I sat up. "No," I said. "Just my purse."

He pulled his pants on and climbed up front. He flicked his cigarette out the window and put his boots on and settled in his seat. Then he touched his finger to his lips, touched the rosary and crossed himself.

He grinned back at me.

"Habit," he said. He started up and shifted into gear..

The Woman in the Wings

True, I'm jealous of my genius boyfriend, true, I resent him at times and at times it must show, though I don't think he notices, I really don't, for a great novelist he's not that perceptive, but to see her badger her poor blind genius husband all through dinner—it was horrible, it made me swear I'd never treat my genius like she treated hers.

It was a shame she had to ruin our ex-patriots' Thanksgiving dinner in Costa Rica. I was excited when my boyfriend told me about the invitation to dine with the famous artist and his infamous wife—she was as well-known as he was, he'd made her so in hundreds of paintings over some forty years—I was sure they'd both be fantastic personalities but what letdowns they turned out to be. It was a shame our Thanksgiving dinner had to be so miserable, I had only a few days with my boyfriend and I wanted to make the most of them. He was staying at an artist colony in a village not far from the famous artist's mansion, Costa Rica is so small nothing is too far from anything else, and I'd flown down to see him. I hadn't seen him in two months, that's how long he had been there (and he was staying one more), slaving away on his second novel but to him such work is not slavish, to him novel-writing is the easiest thing in the world, it makes me sick, at the same time it's what I admire about him most.

The famous artist had invited us himself, or rather had invited my boyfriend, being a famous writer or a writer well on his way to fame gets him all kinds of invitations I don't get. I was just his tag-along, I could only hope they'd made allowance for a guest in the kitchen as they hadn't at the table, when we arrived only three plates were set. Apparently he hadn't told them I was coming, on the drive there he said he couldn't remember if he had or not, it was a stupid thing to do but typical of him, geniuses are forgetful, they're always preoccupied with the grand or grandiose ideas constantly streaming through their heads, they can't help it. I don't hold such minor thoughtlessnesses against him, they're innocent enough, my boyfriend loves me and I'd hate to distract him, any one of those constantly streaming grand ideas could turn out to be a masterpiece and I'd hate to be responsible for depriving the world of it. The last thing I want is to go down in history as one of those women in the wings who bitched and bullied and badgered her genius into obscurity if not the grave. I'd hate for the literary anthologies to say of me in my boyfriend's biographical paragraph "she was the only thing that stood in his way" or "he could really have made a contribution had it not been for her constant bitching and selfish demands." I don't want to go down in history like she, Grete Grausen, the artist's horrible wife, will. Still sometimes I can't help it, I resent my boyfriend and it's gotten worse since his novel made such a big splash, now he's getting all this attention and making all this money (he's proven that even novelists can make money, it's incredible) and I'm still slaving away on my anthropology doctorate even though anthropology really doesn't interest me anymore, I'm sick of analyzing goat's hair death masks and I'm sick of being the woman in the wings. The worst thing is that my boyfriend deserves the rewards he's reaping, he *is* a genius and I'm jealous of him—that's natural enough, those with mediocre talents always envy those with extraordinary ones.

Who knows, maybe Grete Grausen was sick of being the woman in the wings too and that's what made her so mean, maybe after forty years in her husband's shadow she had had enough. Grausen, a fitting name, it means "shivers" or "horrors" in German, she gave me the shivers all right, when we see what we most fear or detest in ourselves taken to grotesque proportions in someone else it really puts us on edge. She'd never taken Lind's last name—that's the artist, you've probably heard of him, he's one of the most famous artists in America and in Europe since 1950, then again Americans don't know anything about artists, very few can name a single one since 1950, it's a shame if not a tragedy—and that was unusual for her generation, perhaps she thought taking his name would interfere with her own fame or perhaps they'd agreed together it was the best way to market her. She'd become a celebrity in her own right, that is, his paintings had made her one, and doubtless her movie star face helped sell them, her eyes were now shriveled and her skin shot but she'd once been stunningly beautiful, blond, blue-eyed, tall and strong-boned, and photos of her in younger days were always printed alongside Lind's paintings in magazines and coffee table books or exhibited alongside them in galleries. The two of them knew how to make money—Lind had been a successful developer on Long Island before being blinded by a flying hammer on the construction site he was strolling through smoking a cigar like the lord of the manor, the hammer shot it out of his mouth like a torpedo, incredibly someone caught it on camera and the photograph later became famous. The flying hammer hit him in the head or rather the brainstem, severing the optic nerve and plunging him into permanent darkness, and yet his curse turned out to be his blessing, at the same time he was struck with blindness he was struck with a gift, the outer eye of the ordinary capitalist replaced by the inner eye of the visionary (no pun intended) artist. It was like an anointing from God, like Paul on the road to Damascus, before being blinded Lind had never picked up a crayon. Some people luck out, their curses turn out to be blessings, others are just cursed but worst of all is to be neither blessed nor cursed but so mediocre fate hardly bothers with you. Maybe Grausen wished she'd been anointed by God instead of her husband, maybe in the twilight of her life (and his, they were both well into their seventies) she was coming out of his shadow, out of the shadow and into the twilight—we often wait until the end of our lives to do things we should have done in the beginning, and yet we always eventually do them, we don't have as much control over our secret desires as we like to think, our secret desires always get the best of us, it's only a matter of time.

The artist met us at the door of his mansion himself. It's a pretentious word, even old-fashioned, "mansion," but it's the right one. The front portico was raised on marble pillars at least two stories high, a Henry Moore sculpture sat in a fountain on the front lawn amid tropical plants with huge, geometric blooms, the cut Venetian glass doors were twelve-feet high and five wide. Inside the architecture was Spanish style, they were tasteful ex-patriots or wanted people to think they were, their choice of architecture suggested their respect for the native culture: narrow corridors cut with delicate arches, white adobe walls, mosaic floors, a tiled central courtyard (where dinner was served) populated by tropical flora and exotic birds stuffed into antique brass cages. Lind's art had really done him well or rather his blindness had—that flawedness was what made him so famous, not that his work was mediocre, it wasn't, his natural talent was obvious, but a blind painter is fantastic if not unexplainable. The public, especially the American public, loves the fantastic like nothing else, they're bored to death with rational materialism and it's at the root of the psychological malaise of our time (my boyfriend's words, I agree). The American public loves novelties like Jacek Lind, you must have heard of him, he's actually been on *Ripley's Believe It or Not*, that's the only kind of artist the American public pays attention to, the flashy, oddball kind. Lind was Polish-American but not Jewish, thank god, that would have been too much, we would have been seeing a Hitlerian reenactment right before our eyes, the Aryan goddess heckling and humiliating the helpless Jew, they made an odd enough couple as it was.

The blind artist led us inside, his fingers trailing on the narrow adobe corridors, he didn't carry a cane, his fingertips must have grown their own eyes through years of guiding the brush over the canvas. I'd expected the mansion to be plastered with his paintings, I'd been looking forward to seeing more of his work, but the million-dollar walls were bare, perhaps he'd grown tired of snagging his fingers on them and had them removed, sometimes practical considerations outweigh lofty ones. He didn't strike me as a genius, he struck me as an old man in houseslippers, though they were leather, probably Italian, millionaires favor Italian shoes. He wore a green silk robe loosely tied but I didn't find it sloppy or off-putting, beneath he was fully dressed in dress shirt and trousers (but no tie, in the tropics dress along with everything else is more casual). Lind's most distinct feature was not his glassy, ghostly gaze, but the monstrous hump rising from his back. A mound the size of a small pumpkin swelled between his shoulders, making his head jut forward and his gaze fall to the floor, where it was nearly impossible to meet. Of course in his case it didn't matter, it was even a relief not to have to meet that gaze, no one wants to look into blind eyes, it feels like a breach of privacy, like accidentally glimpsing someone's private parts when their clothes slip, it feels perverse.

Lind led us to a sunlit room with a wall of glass doors that opened onto the courtyard in which I could see the dinner table set for three but he couldn't and so wasn't embarrassed by it. After my boyfriend introduced himself by all three of his names and me by only one of mine (the first, though it was preceded by my prestigious title, that is, ". . . and this is my girlfriend, T—a"), we stood in an awkward triangle. There was an awkward pause. My boyfriend brought out his novel, when things get tense he brings out his novel. He held it out to Lind (uselessly, the blind are hard to get used to). 'There's no braille version yet,' he said, 'I'm hoping they'll do one, but for now I'd like to offer you my new novel' ("new," he might as well have said "latest," he was obviously implying he'd written others when in fact this was his first). 'Oh,' said Lind pleasantly, his lizard head jerking forward unconsciously, 'I'm honored.' 'I meant to bring you my book of short stories too—another time, or I could mail it to you.' 'Oh,' Lind echoed himself. 'Thank you. I'm honored.' His voice was thin and scratchy, his aged lungs running short on air, and his words emerged slowly as if they had picked up the cautiousness his feet had learned from years of stepping through darkness. My boyfriend nudged his book at his curled fingers, you could almost see the ghostly brush they'd clenched all those years, they uncurled and took it, lucky for him he couldn't see its creepy Norman Rockwell cover. 'Bryce tells me you're the finest writer at the colony this year,' Lind said. Bryce was the American director of the artist colony where my boyfriend was staying, he had hooked the two geniuses up. It was not necessarily a kind thing to say, simply protocol for the greater artist to flatter the lesser or the proven genius to tip his hat to the potential one, the other way round would have been too obvious and both of them knew it. My boyfriend laughed. 'I'm sure he hasn't read me.' Lind smiled dimly. 'Well, he may not have. But he says you're getting a lot of attention in the States.' 'This one has gotten some,' my boyfriend said, gesturing at his book (the blind are almost impossible to get used to). 'I mean—my novel, this one'—he gestured spastically—'Ahem,' Lind cleared his throat—'It *is* getting some attention. I'm pretty happy with the reviews. But I try not to think about public—or critical—opinion too much, you know?' His boyish brow furrowed as it does when he's trying too hard. 'I don't think you can, after all you never know what they want. You certainly can't write to it.' Lind smiled serenely, he wasn't too concerned about public opinion either.

Suddenly we heard a shriek: 'Jacek!' It was her, the other half of the legendary couple, the movie star death camp survivor herself. Framed by the arch of the corridor to the kitchen, Grausen stood iron-straight in her big German bones, she had excellent posture for a woman in her seventies, perhaps she learned to stand so upright in the death camps, where if you slouched you were shot. We could hear pots and pans banging behind her, apparently she'd been supervising the cooking of the German Thanksgiving dinner for American guests by Tico servants (she served sauerkraut and sausage as well as turkey and sweet potatoes and plaintains). 'Such look like you roll from the bed, Jacek!' she screeched. 'And your hair, *ach*! At least it suits your pajamas.' In truth the artist hardly had any hair, what whitened strands he did have lay slicked over his brown-spotted skull, I didn't see what was wrong with it. She clapped her hands on her wide hips and looked at my boyfriend. 'Don't expect such like talk from him. Talk of art, talk of books,' she said, scowling, clipping the English words with her sharp German tongue. 'People expect he have something to say, but *never* he have.'

My boyfriend looked at her, his mouth slightly open, at a loss for words, a rarity for the genius writer of a thousand and twelve pages. He was constantly pointing out how long his book was, I never pointed out it was actually a thousand eleven and a bit pages, the thousand-twelfth page didn't even contain a full paragraph.

'It's not the cause his old age, *never* he talked,' Grausen went on. She shook her head violently and tsked her teeth. '*Nein*, you can't get such like one word out from him.' My boyfriend shifted uncomfortably on his feet as she approached. He wouldn't meet my gaze even though I met his or attempted to, I was rolling my eyes in disgust at Grausen's incredible behavior and I wanted him to see me roll them, he should count his blessings I didn't treat him that way. All evening my boyfriend avoided my gaze, I couldn't figure out why and it was enough to drive me crazy. We'd been getting along fine when we arrived.

'Offer our guests to sit, Jacek! Their legs must be tired after climbing on that rotten hill.' Her English was heavily accented, she probably held onto the German sentence constructions and accent deliberately, a perverse form of national pride or a way of making herself more exotic. As for our legs, it's true the mansion sat atop a hill or in Costa Rican terms a mountain, it overlooked the rain forest and village below, a fantastic view for a painter who could see it, but we'd driven right up to the front gates, the walk up to the marble-pillared portico was less than fifty yards. She pointed a long red fingernail at a white leather sofa: 'Sit, sit! Will you take champagne?' She smiled generously, a smile that cracked her wasted face, powdered white plaster of Paris face, she had switched roles from badgering wife to world's greatest hostess. She crossed the room, took Lind's arm, snorting (not uncouthly, it was the German version of a laugh or chuckle, though what was amusing her I don't know), waited for us to sit and then sat down next to him on the second white leather sofa in the room, the furniture was more American millionaire than Spanish style. She crossed her legs and smiled at her husband, too bad he couldn't see her good will. '*Mein Dios*, Jacek,' she said, combining German and Spanish, it sounded ridiculous. She elbowed him in the ribs. 'Cheer up. You look such like your best friend is dead.' As far as I could see, he was wearing the same dumb smile he wore all evening.

He wore that silk housecoat all evening too, apparently even she forgot about it or didn't really care in the first place. By dinner's end, its lapels were stained with the oily tracks of the peas he spilled, a shame, I doubted they'd come out, then again millionaires have whole closets of silk robes. As for Grausen, she wore the complex, fabricky dress "such like" aged women favor, a gold and cream linen, chenille, and silk pantsuit-sari draped with several glittery beige scarves. Aged women think such abstract concoctions distract from their shot looks, their wasted skin and sagging jowls, they forget or are in denial there is no distracting from the wasted face, no clothing or jewelry can resurrect the maiden in the hag. I can't blame them, for women looks are very important, some are convinced it's all they have. I've always felt attractive enough to get the men I want but I'm not so beautiful I intimidate men as Grausen must once have done. She must have survived the camps, I thought, by giving sexual favors to the soldiers, a perverse or irreverent thought, I couldn't help it, maybe I was jealous of her good looks even though they were clearly shot, her thick golden hair now yellow-white puffs that showed her bluish skull, her sky-blue eyes now shriveled in watery mucus. Still I'd never have the movie star looks she'd once had and I'd never be the star subject of a world-famous painter. Grete Grausen had had a hard life, I knew her story well enough before that miserable dinner, had I kept it in mind I may have been more inclined to forgive her her abominable behavior, then again those of us who have never been through such traumas secretly think they're exaggerated, it gets us out of feeling guilty for having had it so easy.

Her husband had made sure we knew her story in his portraits of her in the Nazi death camps. It was uncanny if not eerie how without ever having seen her—he'd been blind when they met, it was another of the fantastic details of their story and couldn't have hurt in making them celebrities—he captured in the shape of her face or the slant of her eyes something unmistakably her own, it must have been that genius inner eye God had anointed him with. He painted her behind glass-topped barbed wire, garbed in rags, skeletal arms stiff at her sides, starved body flat and masculine, typical enough portraits of a death camp prisoner, what made them unique (aside from being rendered by a blind man) was the beauty queen glamour girl face he always topped her off with. The head mushroomed out of the stick-figure body, blown up to grotesque proportions and yet its features were never distorted, they were highly realistic, almost photographic. Coy, sideways-glancing, even seductive cornflower blue eyes with long curling lashes, pursed red lips and china doll white skin—a Marilyn Monroe face poised atop a skeleton. Grausen was purebred Aryan, which made her story even more shocking—she'd spent years in the camps, she went in right at the beginning. What we didn't know was how or why, we found out during that miserable meal but the tale wasn't worth it.

She and I sat on the white leather couches next to our geniuses, our legs crossed, not speaking as we sipped our German champagne (very good, she was quite the patriot, an
ex-patriot patriot, apparently her experience in the camps
hadn't soured her on her country), smiling smiles poor Lind
missed out on, he must have wondered what was going on.
Had we been two women in a competition over the fame or
money of our men she'd have won hands down, no doubt
I think or like to think my boyfriend more famous than he
really is. Besides his collection of short stories (which don't
sell that well and thus don't attract much attention) he's
only written one novel, even if it has made a Big Splash in
the literary world, to put it how my boyfriend's agent is always putting it. Maybe it's the sheer bulk of the book he's
referring to, the paperback is three inches thick and if you
threw it in a lake or, say, a rancid pond, it *would* make a big
splash. My boyfriend is always saying no one has actually
read his novel or if they have they've read only the first five
hundred pages. It doesn't bother him, the first five hundred
are as good as the second and twelve, anyway, it's the rare
reader who can maneuver the linguistic gymnastics and
multi-layered plots the novel's second half lapses into, he
doesn't blame anyone who quits early. Still I'll never tell him
I've only made it to page eight hundred, no matter what he
says he's got an ego about his novel. My boyfriend tries to
keep his ego in check but he tries too hard, it's his obsessive
avoidance of pretense that belies his pretentiousness. Even
if their names come up in conversation he'll refuse to comment on the obscure European or Eastern European writers
everyone knows he's read because they've influenced his
style so heavily, god forbid someone bring up a well-known
writer, if someone brings up Hemingway or Mailer or DeLillo my boyfriend will frantically change the subject to major-
league baseball or global warming rather than be overheard
discussing literature. And he *always*, not just for writerly
occasions, gives all three of his pen name's names, he's so
proud of the pen name he says his agent came up with but
I'm sure he had a hand in himself, it's one of those names in
fashion for male writers these days: three (minimum) boy-

ish, all-American first names like David Sean Anthony or Michael Wallace Taylor, such wholesome names appeal to the American public—if it likes its artists flashy and oddball it likes its writers wholesome and hip, my boyfriend is both. I won't give his names here, you may have heard of him and I don't want to cause trouble or put a dent in his "cult following" which according to his agent the Big Splash established practically overnight. He deserves all the fame he's gotten and the doubtless more to come.

I like my boyfriend's novel, I do, I think it's a work of genius even if I've only made it to page eight hundred. I didn't quit because I was bored, it's just a really long book, even the critics' reviews skim over the last bits, I'd love to quiz one of them on the details of the final chapters. But I feel a pang of jealousy every time I see the two and a half shelves full of it on my bookcase with its creepy Norman Rockwell cover (it's supposed to caricature the book's screwed up characters with their "unmistakably American existential malaise" to lift a line from the back cover). I've always thought there was something repulsive if not pathological about Rockwell's paintings, they're perfectly suited to *The Saturday Evening Post* but not to great literature, that cover was the worst aesthetic choice if not the worst career move my boyfriend's ever made . . . A few months before he went to Costa Rica, my boyfriend moved in with me, keeping his apartment on the other side of the city, that is, San Francisco, which according to his agent is the third best town for up-and-coming writers behind, of course, New York and L.A. He kept his apartment to write in, it's not that he couldn't write, he said, when I was around (I'm home a lot, my coursework is completed and this year is devoted to my dissertation), it's that when he wrote at my place he was always worrying that I was bored, he always felt like I was lurking in the other room (my words, not his) waiting for him to get done so we could walk down to the coffeeshop or catch an art film together. Maybe I was, I'm so sick of goat's hair death masks I can hardly stand it . . .

I'm not jealous of his "cult following" or the women who are constantly e-mailing and calling him, sometimes on my phone, he's been on all the Bay area talk shows and he's not bad-looking. He has a boyish, all-American face (my boyfriend is from Minnesota), even freckles, they clash with his hipster black-frame cat's eye glasses, it's a look lots of women go for. I don't mind, I don't have an insecure bone in my body when it comes to other women, it's his genius I'm jealous of, then to find when I arrived in Costa Rica he'd already finished the first draft of his second novel, he whipped it out hours, he said, before my plane landed, he wanted to get it done so he could give all his attention to me for my four-day, five-night visit, I had to give him credit for that. My boyfriend had already accomplished what he came to Costa Rica to do and he still had a month left. He always gets done what he says he's going to, it's maddening, I've always been more fly-by-the-seat-of-my-pants and that's probably what my boyfriend likes about me most.

Before we had even gotten out of the airport the night I arrived, the night before our miserable Thanksgiving dinner, he announced he'd finished the first draft of the second masterpiece. I couldn't believe it, last I knew he'd been leafing through Barnum and Bailey archives looking for ideas for his Depression era novel about the circus family wandering poverty-ravaged America. But I was happy for him. I even suggested we stop before leaving San José and have a drink to celebrate.

In the smoky, strip-mall café with candles on the table the waiter never lit despite my boyfriend's repeated requests and the sick-sweet mingle of ceviche marinating and plantain frying in the back kitchen, we held hands across the table, hands and gazes, that night my boyfriend couldn't get enough of my gaze, we stared into each other's eyes and talked softly about the last two months. 'I can't believe all the work I'm getting done,' he said. 'That's good. That's wonderful, darling.' (I like to call him "darling" in an old-fashioned, parodic way, I don't if he likes it or not.) 'I get started first thing in the morning, some days I'm at my desk before dawn. I don't daddle around like I used to.' He must have been talking about the habit we'd developed since he moved in of messing around in bed in the mornings, sometimes for half an hour, sometimes longer and sometimes we'd have our coffee and read the newspaper in bed and then go back to messing around. He took a deep breath and puffed out his chest like Tarzan or Popeye, he wouldn't like the reference but that's how he looked. 'And I don't stop until dark. I've never felt so . . . *vital.*' 'Maybe it's the rain forest. Negative ions.' He shook his head. 'No, no, I mean as a writer. I finally have time to just focus on my work, you know? Nothing to distract me. No phone, no web, no cable.' (My boyfriend has a weakness for cooking shows, it's one of the things I find endearing about him.) 'I've finally got, as Woolf put it, a room of my own.' With his free hand he lifted his sangria and sipped from it. He stopped mid-sip. 'I've never even read that,' he added, obviously seized by the terror he was being pretentious. 'But the gist of it—I don't know if you know it—' 'I do,' I said, '—is that a writer's got to have privacy, solitude, a space of his own in order to get any work done. Or her own.' He smiled. 'Really Woolf's argument is for women, but you can hardly think she'd exclude men from having the same needs.' You could, I wanted to say, you could think that and she did exclude them and *I* had read it. But I didn't want to ruffle the waters, my boyfriend's very argumentative and I wasn't in the mood, not over such a minor issue and not on our first night together again. He stroked my hand. Nor did I tell him I've tried every room in my apartment and still can't write my dissertation, I've been on goat's hair death masks for months and that's only chapter four. Nor did he ask about my dissertation, maybe he knows I'm not that interested in anthropology anymore, I doubt it, most men, especially geniuses, can't see past the ends of their noses when it comes to other people, the genius's vision penetrates ultimate reality but when it comes to what's right in front of their noses they're even blinder than the rest of us. My boyfriend probably thinks just because I still have tribal batiks and fertility staffs from third-world countries hanging on my apartment walls anthropology is my passion just as writing is his but what he doesn't know is I'd rather be an artist or a writer like him. I'd never tell him that, I can't risk him guessing my jealousy, anyway I have absolutely no artistic talent or, worse, just enough to be called mediocre, it's one of the great regrets of my life. Instead I go out with artistic men, I've dated folk musicians and painters and a couple of mimes. I even slept with a ballet dancer once, one of the few one-night stands of my life, I thought it worth it for a ballet dancer even though he was mediocre both on stage and in bed. My three-named writer is the most gifted so far. It's a blessing the public has noticed it while he's still young.

When our champagne glasses were dry Grausen ushered us into the courtyard where a rectangular glass table long enough for a banquet was set for three, she noticed right away and barked in German-tinted Spanish at a maid to set another place. The squawks and screeches of the giant trop-ical birds swinging in cages around the pentagonal court-yard reverberated on the tile. Grausen took her seat at the head of the table and started in listing the ten or twelve birds' names, ages, species and personality quirks one by one, they were all named after 1940s German movie stars. The sun was out and the huge, colorful tropical blooms glistened with rainwater from the afternoon shower, it was a beautiful Thanksgiving evening. No one said grace, they weren't that kind of people, we weren't either. Grausen sat Lind on her left and I on his left, my boyfriend alone on the other side. The seating gave him plenty of opportunities to meet my gaze, opportunities he didn't take once, all night he avoided my gaze, either I'd done something to offend or embarrass him or he was simply preoccupied with his own private obsessions, who knows.

Grausen never did introduce herself, perhaps her ego was so puffed up she didn't think it was necessary (it wasn't), nor did she show any desire to know our names. When the turkey arrived, she stood and plunged an enormous pearl-handled fork into it, then went at it with a matching knife the size of a small sword. Now she was playing the man of the house, she cut big steaming planks and placed them on our plates, on her own she put a sliver about the length and breadth of her little finger. 'It's incredible to eat like this,' she said. 'I can't believe such food. I feel sick to my stomach to look at it.' The table was spread with sweet potatoes and mashed potatoes, bratwurst and sour-creamed peas and black German bread, coconut soup, fried plantain and jerk-seasoned swordfish, an outrageous feast topped off with champagne, white wine, and black tea with cream. 'You feel guilty,' Lind said, surprisingly—he'd hardly spoken since she arrived. 'You can't believe you have the right to fill your stomach.' She scowled. '*Ach, nein*, Jacek. Three years was I in the camps, never *once* I feel guilty, why should I feel guilty now?' 'You shouldn't,' he agreed. 'Nobody who was in the camps should feel guilty.' Grausen snapped back, contradicting herself for the sake of contradicting him, it was comical: 'Ha! Easier said than done. Sometimes such you feel guilty, you can't help, or you don't know *how* you feel guilty but you do. You don't know how was it, Jacek. You know *nothing* how was it!' Under his hump Lind's ghostly gaze fixed or appeared to fix on the steaming plate she'd loaded for him. Then, to us: 'Which like I tell him for forty years.' And finally, to herself or to her turkey, she murmured into her plate: 'Such horrors, you can't imagine.'

Still my boyfriend didn't raise his gaze to meet mine across the table or roll his eyes so we could commiserate together or show our incredulity at the famous couple's juvenile behavior even though any other couple would doubtless have done so. He too had fixed his eyes on his turkey, now all three pairs of eyes were on the bird though only two could see it. He took a long slow sip of wine, set his glass down deliberately, and said, 'How did you come to be in the camps, Ms. Grausen, if you don't mind the question?'

She waved her huge, heavily jeweled hand. 'It's what everyone wants to know when they meet me. They think no one like me was in the camps.' She snorted. 'Some don't believe I *was* there, they think like I lie—and Jacek too, in his paintings lying!—They say, *You*? No one like you went' ("vent," really she had a strong accent, it made her a caricature, the fierce, fuming German). 'Like they will catch me in my make believe, like I forget to look in the mirror when I make believe. People are so stupid, *ach*, people give me a headache.' She clapped her hand on her forehead, she was quite the actress. 'But I tell you what happen, such you won't believe. Such stupid mistake, the stupid of the German police ruin my life. I lived in a house on the third floor, my neighbor below me she worked for the underground, everyone in the house knew it. She was smuggling secret papers to the French resistance, such things as get you shot. This was in Berlin, early in the war, a terrible time. Everyone was frightened, everyone but me, I had my head in the clouds, I was on my way to being big actress and my mind always was on stage. I was going to be a star. I should have paid more attention because I looked just like my spy neighbor. We wore our hair the same and we were same like blond, people said we looked like sisters, I thought, what, we both have blond hair, every woman in Berlin has blond hair, every free woman, the problem was we wore it the same way, always I wore my hair in braids long down to my waist, she too wore such hair though hers was not as long as mine and her braids were more thin. A woman would have known us apart no mistake but the police are made of men. One day some fat chief say arrest a woman with blond braids who lives on the third floor of my house, that's what went wrong, the spy lived on the second floor and I on the third in the room over her room, you see what happened, still it's impossible to understand, my life ruined by some stupid police's mistake. Of course, *my* stupid mistake was to keep my hair like the spy's, everyone in the house knew her time was coming, but I was nineteen, my head full with clouds and I such vain with my hair, after all it was very beautiful and won me lots of roles. I had the star role in *Edelweiss* but this I never got to play, the police came for me on opening night.' Her large bony fingers picked at the yellow-white spirally puffs on her skull, cotton candy hair. 'This—it's not my hair was then,' she said absently, and I felt a surge of pity for her. It quickly went away.

'Couldn't you show them your papers, your identification?' I said.

'*Ach*, you don't know how was it, no one but was there knows how was it. These police don't interest in papers. They break your door, they throw you down and beat you. To women they do worse. Such horrors you can't imagine.'

The table was quiet. Grausen gazed down its length as if at a ghost sitting at the opposite end, perhaps the ghost of one of those soldiers or policemen she'd had to please with her body to survive. She hadn't touched her food, those little child-portion piles must be cold by now.

'She never forgets,' said Lind. Grausen: 'His rotten paintings don't *let* me forget.' She glared at him (apparently even she forgot he was blind at times). Lind: 'She's never been that fond of them. They bring back the painful memories.' They were referring to each other in the third person as if they weren't sitting right next to each other or as if my boyfriend and I were judge and jury. Grausen: 'There's no bringing back, such memories *never* go. And it's *I* who has to look at them, he has never to look at his rotten creations.' Lind smiled placidly. 'It's true,' he said. 'I've always given her credit for that, she's provided all my material for me. I'm forever indebted to my wife.' '*Hrmph!*' Grausen snorted.

Lind had been trying with no luck to scoop his few remaining sour-creamed peas onto his fork, a difficult enough task for the sighted. Now he laid his fork down, resorting to his fingers, they groped the plate for the greasy peas. Grausen gasped as if sighting one of those horrors such as she could never forget and we could never imagine and shrieked: '*Ach*, Jacek!'

The peas were already on the way to his mouth and would have made it there safely had she not shouted—her shrill voice must have hammered his super-sensitive ears, the blind develop canine hearing—his hand jumped and the peas shot out, bounced off his green silk lapel and onto the white silk placemat. They rolled a bit and stopped, leaving oily tracks in their wake. Grausen: '*Mein Dios.*' She put her hand to her forehead and closed her eyes. In a low voice she said, 'Jacek, one day your rotten manners will send our guests running to the forest, one day they'll stop coming and then what? Then we'll rot away in these walls, that's what.'

I glanced at my boyfriend. He was shoveling in his sauerkraut like Grete Grausen must have done on Liberation Day, I'd never seen him so famished, men can't stand the slightest tension. I could see if I didn't want to listen to her bitching and badgering her poor husband all through the dinner I'd have to take charge, I wasn't going to miss this opportunity to talk to a world-famous artist. I smiled at him, forgetting the absurdity of trying to flatter a blind person with a pleasant smile, and said, 'Are you still painting, Mr. Lind?'

The genius cleared his throat with some effort as was his habit, he had a problem with phlegm, we could hear it gurgling in there. 'Not really. I do have several paintings, oh, you know, in progress'—he chuckled, his other habit was this self-deprecatory chuckling, he really had no backbone, no wonder he was a humpback. And, of course, he was a perfect target for her—I imagined that pumpkin-sized hump beneath his neck was filled with Grausen's cruelties and cut-downs. He jutted his chin in my direction but his gaze slid past mine to land somewhere in the wreckage of food, overflowing dishes we hadn't touched and wouldn't—'I call them my stillborns, they'll never be completed, not at this late hour.' He wasn't talking about the evening, I wondered how it must feel, the inevitable approach of the twilight. For him the darkness had fallen years ago but soon a darker and even more permanent darkness would descend. 'And my hands, they're on their way out too, they ache after ten minutes. But my worst enemy is my back. As you can see it gives me trouble, it's very painful.'

'Kyphosis,' barked Grausen. 'The popular word is hunch-back.' She turned to me as if to an ally or confidant, per-haps it had just dawned on her I was a woman too, women among men instinctively feel some camaraderie. 'If he'd sit in his chair—the beautiful chair his chiropractor sent from Switzerland, thirty thousand we spend on this chair, and *there* he refuses to sit!' She pointed through the Spanish style arches where indeed the chair was parked in the patio shadows, like a space alien or science fiction creature with its steel spires and clamps and hooks and vast computer panel. 'Look! It sits—and you know where *he* sits? There'— she pointed to a weather-worn stone bench, backless, at the far side of the courtyard. 'He works on that old bench—if you call his silly sketches work—it's incredible. He will do *nothing* what's good for him, he'd rather give up working than take care his back. People think he's superman, he's not, he's a stubborn old goat. I think he's done with art, I think he *wants* to quit.'

I swallowed my sweet potatoes. Everyone else was taking the chance to swallow or chew or sip, too. I said, 'Oh, you're working on some sketches?'

Lind either ignored me or didn't hear me. 'She may be right,' he said. 'To tell the truth I don't have that many ideas any-more. Nothing really comes to me, I can't see like I used to. I could paint my wife until the end of my days, I never tire of her as my subject but you can hear how tired she is of being my subject and I don't want to paint her if she doesn't want me to. Even artists have to respect others' wishes, even they have to face the fact they don't rule the world.' It was the most he'd said all night and I felt vaguely charmed, but he capped it off with one of those disgusting self-conscious throat clearings, he brought up some phlegm he'd later have to put back down. He added, 'When they're really working on something artists think they rule the world, it feels fine at the time but later they pay for it.'

'Pay? How?' my boyfriend said. He was perking up, the conversation was finally starting to interest him.

Lind waved his hand as if erasing or attempting to erase his words, a gesture so like Grausen's it was eerie. 'Oh, I don't know. Ahem, ahem.' He put the phlegm back down where it belonged. 'Is the turkey tender enough for you?'

'It's very good,' my boyfriend said.

'But maybe it won't be the same for you.' Lind chuckled, he wasn't talking about the turkey. 'Maybe you'll be the one who gets away with it.'

Now it was my boyfriend's turn to clear his throat. He shifted in his seat. 'Get away with what?'

Lind's eyelids fluttered over his glassy eyes. He sat back in his chair and his lizard head sank into his shoulders. He sighed. 'Did I tell you I'm working on some sketches?' Again he either evaded or ignored the direct question—while, ironically, answering my earlier one.

'Those such he does on his bench,' said Grausen with her mouth full, she'd finally taken a few morsels of her sweet potatoes and was chewing at them for all she was worth, but she couldn't let the opportunity to take a jab at him pass by.

'I don't have any new ideas but I do have a new friend. I'm getting to know the pencil again, I've been spending my mornings with it, it's a wonderful instrument though I use only one end. I don't make mistakes, I can't see them if I do, so for me they don't exist.' He frowned thoughtfully. 'May I show you? No one but Grete's seen them.'

On the drive up we'd fantasized Lind would invite us to his studio, show us masterpieces no eyes had yet lain upon, it would really be something to tell our friends, Lind is one of the most famous artists in America as well as in Europe since 1950. We nodded enthusiastically.

'They're nodding,' Grausen told him irritably. Then, to us: 'Don't get excited. They're not much. If he'd sit in his chair he might make something but he perches on that rotten bench such like a mountain goat, I don't know why, he can't even see the view.' (A shame, Lind missed out on his own million-dollar view of the rainforest.) 'One day he'll catch cold sitting in that dew, he's sitting there at the break of dawn, it's incredible, scratching the air with his kindergarten pencil. One day I'll find him freezen on the grass—he's been stubborn all his life and such stubborn will put him in the grave, he's almost there now, look at him, seventy-seven, it's too old to sit in the dew on such a bench.'

'And I didn't expect to live to be sixty,' Lind said.

Grausen stabbed her last shred of turkey. 'You should sit in your chair.'

Lind grinned. 'Not bad for a hunchback.'

Grausen: 'You're not the typical hunchback.' It was almost a compliment. She popped the turkey in her mouth, a bite no bigger than a fingernail. Then she went at her plate with a finger, wiping it clean and licking her finger down to the red-painted manicured nail until not a crumb or trace or smear of food was left.

When the pumpkin pie with great dripping dollops of rum-flavor whipped cream (which Grausen skipped in favor of more champagne) had been served and eaten and the Tico maid was clearing the table, Grausen snapping orders at her from her throne at its head, Lind shuffled off for his sketches, his fingers groping the open air until he reached the security of the adobe walls. My boyfriend's gaze was roaming the courtyard, at last it settled on one particular bird, I think it was Marlene Deitrich. Apparently he preferred the sight of animal cruelty to the sight of my eyes—the magnificent birds were stuffed in cages half their size and they obviously didn't like it, their screeches and squawks had hammered our eardrums all night, echoing Grausen's even more painful screeches and squawks. I reached across the table to get my boyfriend's attention, a last resort. At last he looked at me. I rolled my eyes as if to say "can you believe these two," it was the private exchange any couple would indulge in in such a situation, and we finally did, he rolled his eyes back and covered my hand with his. Out of the corner of my eye I saw—or thought I saw, the inner eye too has its grand delusions and shapes or censors what the outer eye sees—Grausen's gaze start when it fell on our joined hands. She went right on bickering with the maid but I thought I saw her gaze start or twitch when it fell on our shameless exhibition of camaraderie or sexual attraction or true love the way one's gaze does when it meets something it fears or detests or envies such as the obvious affection between my boyfriend and myself.

True, I'm in love with my boyfriend, it's hard not to fall in love with a man whose art you genuinely admire. His work is nothing like Lind's, it's not personal at all, my boyfriend is a razor's edge, no-holds-barred social critic or allegorist and he doesn't let his private obsessions or secret desires leak into his work. I don't recognize anyone from my boyfriend's real life in his novel, including myself, I'm not insulted because I didn't know him when he was writing it. But I wonder if anyone else in his life is insulted not to feature in his masterpiece, his mother or sisters or former girlfriends, women are more picky about that sort of thing, or at least more inclined to bring it out in the open if they are insulted. Everyone envies the position of Grete Grausen, nothing is more flattering than to be the star subject of a loved one's art.

I looked at him as I held his hand in the dimming twilight, suddenly I felt very in love with him and was glad I'd come to visit. I looked at his too-short prep school haircut with the long, fashionable bang that fell over one eye and gave him the hipster if not indie-rock look (he was already thirty-seven, barely young enough to be considered a promising young writer), he thought it important to market himself as a hip young writer, indeed his agent had recommended the cut. His black-framed cat's eye glasses and thick lips contrasted with his boyish freckles and pudgy, farmboy face—my boyfriend is from Duluth, a fact he's embarrassed to relate now most of his time is spent between New York and San Francisco. What if I was, I thought, the star subject of his new novel. What if our relationship has leaked into his work in spite of himself, it's only a matter of time before our secret obsessions slip through the cracks, we don't have as much control over them as we like to think. Perhaps he'd made me the heroine of his story about the Depression era circus family wandering poverty-ravaged America in caravan wagons, battling tornadoes, tuberculosis, railroad hobos and swindlers (it sounded a lot like the *Grapes of Wrath* to me but I didn't dare tell him that, he knows as well as I do the last thing literature needs is another *Grapes of Wrath*). That would explain why he'd been so vague describing it over our sangria at that strip-mall café the night before, not because the moment I got off the plane he'd regretted inviting me and was thinking what a drag it was going to be to share his room of his own with me for the next five nights and how even sex wasn't worth it. He'd probably been so vague so I wouldn't guess my role in the new masterpiece, but I doubted I was the heroine or the love interest, that would be too obvious for my boyfriend, more likely I was the fishnet-stockinged lion tamer who sticks her head in the lion's mouth once too far or the beautiful but clumsy trapeze artist whose gloves slip mid-pinwheel. My boyfriend likes to see me as a fly-by-the-seat-of-my-pants, devil-may-care kind of girl (and maybe I am one), flighty and foolish, that's the kind he goes for, but he's always warning me if I'm not careful I'm going to hurt myself one of these days . . .

Lind shuffled back with the sketches, sat down and held them out in the direction of my boyfriend, who took the top few pages, they were on plain white drawing paper, eleven by fourteen it looked like, and handed me (a rare moment of thoughtfulness) the rest, there were six or seven. They were blank. There was nothing there, or not that I could see. For a split second it occurred to me my eyes were tainted simply by being feminine, that Lind's latest genius must be accessible only to the male gaze, after all my boyfriend was examining them intensely, holding them so close to his face I couldn't see if they too were blank. At last he lowered them, and there was nothing but some grayish smudges that looked like the oils fingerprints inevitably leave on white paper once they've handled it a few times.

'They're experimental,' Lind was saying. 'I'm trying something new with the pencil.'

Maybe he's using the wrong end, I thought. He said he only uses one end. I looked at Grausen. She met my eyes and shrugged. She frowned. 'Never I understood art,' was all she said. Then she turned and looked out at the million-dollar view, her eyes far away in her wasted face.

'Very interesting,' my boyfriend murmured. He was gazing intensely at the blank pages as if his own inner eye had just opened up.

Grausen was the one who called it a night. 'It's 9:30, I like him to bed by nine,' she said. Lind told her feebly, 'I want to be up at dawn.' He smiled in our general directions. 'You've inspired me. I think I'll finish these tomorrow.' He stood, his hump rising up like a beast hidden in him all this time. He extended his hand across the table and my boyfriend took it. 'Come see me again,' he said. 'I'll read your book and we can talk about it.' 'I have a lot to do this week,' Grausen snarled. 'Francisco will have to read it to you.' 'Sure, Francisco will read it to me,' said Lind, then to my boyfriend and it seemed to me there was some cryptic message concealed in his froggy voice, some secret code meant only for the two of them: 'Come back. Come in the afternoon. We have a lot to talk about, we didn't scratch the surface tonight.'

It was a depressing evening. We were quiet on the drive back to the colony, indeed the whole weekend was quiet if not depressing, that miserable dinner set the tone for the rest of my visit, even the sex wasn't very good. I left wondering if my boyfriend wanted to break up with me and didn't have the guts to do it but my worries turned out to be needless.

My boyfriend has been back from Costa Rica a few months and things are going really well. He never went back to see Lind and he regrets it—Lind died a few weeks after our visit, now he's really famous and becoming even more so, it's one of the blessings of the curse of death. Grausen must be raking in the millions now, the fantastic way he died, fried by an electrical malfunction of the Swiss space alien chair (I could see his blackened hump, his hands eternally "freezen" in those grotesque curls), would really sell paintings. A fantastic way to die, that is, if you didn't know those two, if you'd never had Thanksgiving dinner with them and seen how his woman in the wings was constantly badgering him to sit in his "special chair," now we know why, her secret desires finally got the best of her, it was only a matter of time. That's what I think, my boyfriend doesn't agree, it's amazing how he can render such complex and believable characters and yet be so blind when it comes to real people. It's probably best I'm not in his second novel—now that I've read it I really don't recognize myself, the lion tamer's breasts are too small, the trapeze artist too dim-witted, then again maybe that's how he sees me, we never see ourselves as others do, the inner eye in each of us clouds the outer vision. I love my boyfriend and we're getting along really well. He's in the other room now, when he came back we made it into a study for him and he finally gave up his apartment, apparently he's gotten over worrying about me being bored while he's writing. Either that or he actually thinks I'm writing, too, sitting here in my room of my own with my death mask research scattered about me, he doesn't see my freezen pen or blank page, the signs are right in front of his nose but he doesn't see any of them. His study is nice, sunny, with a wall of glass doors he can look through out to the backyard and on clear days see the Golden Gate, a beautiful view, he says he doesn't take it for granted as he would have before meeting Lind. He's writing now, I can hearing the clicking of his fingers on the keyboard, he's making the final touches on his novel, his agent says it's the best draft he's produced yet. No doubt my boyfriend's on the road to even greater fame and greater genius, it's only a matter of time. His new novel will be on bookshelves (mine and stores' nationwide) before New Year's, the only problem is his first novel has already consumed all the space on my bookshelves, I don't know where I'm going to put all the copies of the new one. If he keeps churning out these monstrous novels, they're going to take over the bookshelves in my room of my own, too. One of these days I'm going to have to do something about it. It's only a matter of time.

nightgown

nightgown

She wakes and listens and does not hear him. He is not moving in his bed that she can hear, not tossing and turning and shifting the strange weight of the cast on the foot that was broken today. She gets up and moves mechanically through the dark hall into the kitchen. The nightgown emerges from the darkness more than she does, with the bigness and contrast of its whiteness. She stops under the unlit bulb and listens again. Still nothing. The bones are delicate at his age. They are still forming, they have years yet before they will be completely shaped. His child bones remind her of chickens' wishbones: they snap easily, but it takes some effort to peel them apart as the sinews stretch and thin, resisting.

She pulls the light cord and the kitchen shocks into light. There is the chew-eared cat lying half on the two-by-four board that levels the refrigerator, pretending to sleep. She has a glass of water and waits. The clean circumference of the nightgown's hem hangs at her ankles, perfectly still. It is so quiet in the country. Quiet that is undivided by anything, whole as an egg cupped in a hand. In this quiet some night there may be a sound, perhaps a cry that is not a coyote's, a call for her that is not her son's, or there may be no call, ever, just one day following another, year stacking upon year.

She listens again toward his room, then hearing nothing goes out the back screen door, whose squeak cracks the quiet. Outside, though, there are nets of sounds, overlapping. The insect-drowned warm weather sounds, the ring of crickets, coons or possums or coyotes rustling the cornfields. And most immediate, the thwup-thwup-thwup-thwup of the nightgown in the wind.

The nightgown is big, truly gownlike. It is white, one hundred percent spun cotton, sheer in direct light. Yellowed lace lines the cuffs and neck and a bib shape on the chest. These ruffles give some pizzazz. Otherwise it's a very plain nightgown, very traditional, very pioneer. Old but the strong fabric shows no signs of wear or time. It may have been her grandmother's or great-grandmother's; she doesn't know, she only remembers finding it in her mother's things when she died. The nightgown is modesty itself: it covers everything. It buttons high on the neck, low on the wrists, hangs beyond the ankles. Her feet, hands, and head sticking out seem a trio of separate, floating parts.

Only ten feet of grass from the back step to where the cornfield spills its spiky waves as far as she can see. She stands on this step in the fluttering nightgown with her hair down fluttering too, looking like a girl, not a mother.

cornfield

The nightgown sweeps her into the rows of corn. It decides on its own. This is how it begins to move: the wind slips beneath the gown and fills the view from her chin with its sail. Inflating beneath her breasts round as a watermelon or a baby in the belly. The back of the gown hugs her calves and fishtails out front between them. Like this it begins to move, and she feels its force, not the force of the wind but the force of the nightgown. Or the spirit in the nightgown.

So into the corn. By a row of dirt between rows of stalks; she follows this row. All the rows are the same, equally spaced and parallel, the spiny stalks repeating and repeating. The corn is higher than her head which is almost as high as it will get—it is September and they will harvest probably next week. The green and black-with-shadow leaves flap and wave and their shadows make watery waves after them. She looks through the waves at the stars and walks in her row.

This is walking from. Not walking to, walking from. She lets her fingers trail, catching and releasing the repeating stalks, catching and releasing, repeating and repeating this simple catching and releasing and walking, walking to nothing and from everything until she has walked so far she has walked through nothing and come to somewhere else. Here she might be a chef instead of a mother. She might cut up fish and patch it with herbs. The other chef would come into the kitchen, shouting. A big, moustached man who was in love with a married woman. His name would be hard to pronounce. He would be the best chef in the world, and she would be next best. Really she would not be a chef. A dancer, perhaps, if she had the body and grace for it. Or a singer or traveler. Then she would never know if the foot healed all right, or if it will make him walk crooked, balanced on one side of it, or whatever else will eventually happen to him.

But when she comes to the end of the field where the trees begin and looks back there is only the field she sees every day out the kitchen window, the daylight field. This is the field the combines will shave clean next week, moving over it like giant bugs; this is corn for harvesting, nothing else. She starts back.

bones

The boy is sleeping. He is sleeping very soundly for how his foot must ache. She can hear his soft, content breathing but she cannot see him well from her position at the side of the house, where she presses her nose into the windowscreen. The room is darker than the outside darkness, but she can make out the corners of his bed, his tiny flat uncovered chest, the faint shine of his towhead and of course the swollen white bulb of the cast on top of the covers. The cast is so small, the size one of his father's socks might have been. The father who is gone and has been gone since before him.

The foot was broken at Sunday School. They had the Bible lesson outside because the air conditioner was broken and the basement windows painted shut. September days still get above ninety, though night temperatures plunge; tonight it is almost chilly. It is a good thing the nightgown covers so thoroughly.

She sat on the picnic table nearby in her jeans, waiting for him. When the teacher said, What should Jonah have done in the first place? her son wasn't listening. His satin white head barely three years old was peering in the space between the picnic table and its bench, which he was sitting on. He was so small, he didn't have to hunch to see there. He was watching threads of fat, red fire ants cross the pavement below his dangling feet.

He should have gone to Nineveh in the first place, huh? the teacher said, and the children all agreed. That's where he ended up anyway. They nodded soberly, they said, uh-huh, all but her son. Then the lesson was over and the other children bolted off to the merry-go-round. When they did, the uneven picnic table shifted onto a different three legs, and her son slid neatly through the space between the table and bench onto the ants. He didn't care; he didn't yet know about ants, and they hadn't begun biting. When he crawled out under the opposite bench and stood up wiping the ants on his jeans, his sneakered foot was under the one table leg that was elevated. She saw it there; she watched every-thing slowly happen. The next moment, the teacher, as if on purpose but of course not, jumped up on the bench and sent the table leg down on his foot. At the same time she saw her son's mouth open and his face warp soundlessly, the Sunday school teacher was clapping her hands and yell-ing at the children to get down off the top spindles of the merry-go-round—it was dangerous up there.

The teacher is a big woman. She, his mother, is small. People compare her to poultry. Her legs do resemble sparrows', her bulletish eyes, too, and her nervousness recalls pecking hens. She is shy and hidden. This is apparent in her quick, irregular movements, because there is something of her that will try to surface from time to time. She has to be fast to cover it before it is observed, if only by herself. But she does what she can; she acts when she feels she needs to. She takes care of him, endlessly.

Together they removed the shoe. The foot was changing color before their eyes, purpling. She tested each toe while the teacher, squatting beside her, held the tiny sneaker and sock in her fleshy palm. He shook his head; he couldn't move any. She pressed her thumb gently along each of the five ridges that ran down the top of the foot until she came to the point where the ridges gapped. This point, taken alone, was nothing so terrible, nothing but a space, a harmless gap that was not there before. What was terrible was how the little white foot, her son's adorable, formerly perfect foot, now folded in half at this gap and the tiny toes hung there limply like raw sausages. Then, lines of red sprouting through the skin in the rectangle shape of the table leg as the foot began to bleed.

She set the foot down and put her hands on his knees. He was looking at her expectantly. He didn't look at all upset, just surprised. He hadn't even cried.

The teacher jogged into the church to call the doctor, who would have to be called out of church himself. He went to the Methodist in town. She picked up her son. Now he would cry. She pressed him into her neck, squeezed his tiny ribcage, kissed his hair. The picnic table leaned, the guilty leg off the ground again. She kicked it awkwardly.

The five bones are still in ten pieces, but they are aligned now so to suggest to them the advantages of becoming five longer, stronger bones again. Under the cast, they are stretching together at this very moment.

The boy has not yet moved in his sleep. He is sleeping so soundly a sounder sleep does not seem possible. Usually a person, usually a child especially, will roll back and forth in bed, and some breaths will be deeper than others, some restless gasps. But this one lies perfectly still and breathes perfectly evenly. His breath is the only evidence he is alive.

How trustingly he lets it move in and out of him, in the softest, most willing of exchanges.

road

The nightgown tugs toward the gravel road that runs before the house. It begins to move, the wind filling it again, in this direction. It does not touch the ground or the branches as it passes. It does not touch her patient, agreeable body. Except maybe a little. Maybe just enough to know that it, the body that has learned the cool and calm of an absent husband's absent fingers, is responsive enough to its touch to come along within it. Maybe in these circumstances this body considers stopping being patient, stopping agreeing. No, it does not; it is a body that has learned to be satisfied with being patient, if this is still patience. This is the body that is transported in the nightgown to the gravel road that shines with not moonlight but in a concentrated pool of mercury light from the wooden pole in the yard.

The nightgown sees the emptiness of the road. It sees this emptiness in the same way her body has learned to see its patience, not as emptiness but as promise that something will eventually happen. The road, too, is a place where something, perhaps not the best thing, but something, will happen.

car

She is sitting in the middle of the road looking up at the stars when the car's headlights find her. There are never any cars on the road at this time of night and hardly any in the day, but somehow she's not surprised to see this one. She stands and moves to the shoulder, her nightgown an upside-down cone around her like a paper Christmas angel. The car slows and stops. The driver, too, she finds as she leans in his window, her hands gripping the inch of glass that has not been rolled down, is just who she expected to see: a stranger, but the familiar kind, one who has, for instance, some qualities she recognizes, such as certain hand gestures he has yet to make, or the angles of his profile.

He turns and looks full at her but doesn't say anything.

Where you headed? she says.

He laughs. Good question. Everyone asks such good questions around here.

Oh? she says. What's a good question?

One with hundreds of answers. And all you can say is, good question, meaning, you know as well as I do.

How would I know where you're going? she says.

Because I'm not going anywhere. Just driving. He hooks a thumb at the passenger seat. Come on, get in. A midnight ride.

Her mouth twists almost into a smile.

You must think I'm crazy, she says, but she doesn't lean back from the window.

The man cocks his head. Maybe just a little?

This time she does smile, and lets him say it: Good question, huh?

Maybe it is the nightgown or the force within the nightgown, she doesn't know, but she finds herself stepping into the headlights to cross to the passenger side. For a second her body is X-rayed through the wind-busy cotton and the bones are there; she is not a paper angel with only air beneath her gown.

The man is wearing a black leather jacket, possibly a sign of trouble but she is not looking for signs. His car smells like lemon air freshener and old cigarette smoke. He accelerates smoothly and the house drops away behind them, and she does not think of her son, who perhaps is waking in the dark house alone, foot throbbing.

She keeps her head turned toward her window, watches the grass blowing in the ditches and the fields of corn passing by. She does not see the roads as much as the fields; fields enfold roads rather than roads cutting up fields in this part of the country, particularly at this season when the corn is so high you are on the intersection before you see it.

At a cattle guard the man stops and takes off his leather jacket and lays it on the seat between them. He takes a cigarette from his shirt pocket and lights it, then switches it to the hand on the steering wheel and lays his other hand on the jacket. The hand lies prone, like a resting animal, the fingers slightly curled.

Ask me another good question, he says as the car moves forward again.

The ease and the bit of crazy she felt standing at the edge of the road leaning into his car is gone.

Okay, she says. But she can't think of anything.

Spontaneously, she rolls down the window all the way and puts her head into the hard-coming wind. Her hair flies and whips her cheeks. She puts her arm out, too, and opens her mouth, lets the wind dry it, as she did when she was a kid. The wind fills the sleeve of the nightgown, making the thwup-thwup-thwup, furiously now. She remembers suddenly what she is wearing, and feels the hot floorboard on her bare soles. She pulls herself back into the car. At least it's pioneer-style, covers everything. She looks at him. He is wearing jeans and a western shirt, unsnapped halfway down his chest. He is holding his cigarette down by his knee.

Sorry, she says, and rolls up the window.

The man ashes out his own cracked window and says, I've got one. What were you doing in the middle of the road in your nightgown?

She looks at him helplessly. I was checking on my son. He's wounded.

Wounded? Was he in a war? He chuckles to himself, then pauses, reconsiders. Was he?

He's three, she says. He broke his foot today.

So he was sleeping in the middle of the road, I see. The man nods, teasing.

She looks at him. She can feel some of the craziness returning, a kind of tingling in her fingers and toes. Yeah, she says, he likes the stars.

Who doesn't? I do. He leans on the window and looks up at the sky.

You can't get him to sleep anywhere but right in the middle of the road, she says, then, with an almost physical shock, she remembers. She sits up.

You'd better take me back. He might've woken up.

They have flown past several intersections, which mark half-mile fields. So they are already miles from her house.

The dark is whole and solid in the east over the fields, and the man is holding the engine steady, thrusting the car forward as if into deep space.

Why don't you take me back, she says again. She tries to say it carelessly, like what-the-hell, like this choice is no more desirable than any other.

The man lets off the accelerator; the sound of the engine drops. He pulls into the gravel at the side of the road and stops the car. He turns it off. All looking straight out the windshield, never at her.

Now he faces her. He moves the leather jacket from between them, puts it in the back. Then he reaches for her shoulders, half-turns her to him, and puts his hands over both her ears. Removes one hand to put the index to his mouth.

Shhh. He lifts the other hand. Listen.

She hears the night buzzing of crickets and cicadas and mosquitoes and the soft travel of the wind through the stalks, the same sounds she heard not long ago on the back step. His hands are on her shoulders, fingers hot and a little damp through the sheer cotton. She strains to listen, she really does. She doesn't want to think what she already knows, not yet.

His face big in her own, eyes black and big as a horse's, she whispers and she does not think she has kept the fear out of her voice very well: Are you crazy?

No, he says—too fast and too loud. Are you?

She whispers: I just want to know if you're going to hurt me.

He doesn't say anything. But his hands on her shoulders become heavier, as if he has released their full weight. He drops them slowly down her arms, pushing the air out of the puffy sleeves. Then he places one, then the other, flat on her breasts. He slides them to her belly and grips her hips. Then moves them down her thighs, her skinny thighs rising in his palms. His palms are warm if somewhat hard, calloused. He clacks her knees together. The bones make a sound like pool balls cracking. He brings his mouth to her ear, his damp, heated breath.

What's under there? His voice turns hoarse, deep. What's under that granny cape?

Knees, she says, deadpan. She feels him nod, his wiry hair brushing her face. She goes on: And legs.

I get the idea, he says, his grip increasing.

Then his hands move fast back up her thighs and clamp onto her ribs. He pulls her to him and she doesn't resist; she is surprised she doesn't resist. The nightgown has crumpled like air when he pulled her to him and inside the gown she has crumpled, too.

His mouth breathes the stale cigarette taste into hers. But beneath the taste his tongue is warm and thick and familiar, the way it pushes apart the space in her mouth, the way it wants in. Her own hands move jerkily to the chest hair in his open shirt. It is bristly soft. He moves his body up against her. The bones of his gums come hard against hers.

She pulls back. Stop, she says.

Of course, he does not. He comes at her again with his open mouth. She pulls back against the door and he follows, grasping for her. She fumbles for the door handle, finds it, the door springs open and she stumbles into the ditch then out the other side into the cornfield. She runs down the row, fighting through the rubbery leaves and snapping stalks until she's out of breath. Then she squats in the dirt and rests, trying to listen over her breath. She doesn't hear him coming.

After a while she hears him call her. He's not close.

Hey! Hey, come on. I'll take you back. No sweat. Come on back.

She stands and looks through the sword-tops of the stalks. He's standing at the edge of the field, probably a hundred yards away, squinting into it with his hands on his hips. She gets her first look at him out of the car. He's short, and older than she'd realized.

He slaps his hands on his thighs. I'm serious! I promise. I'll take you straight back. No funny business. It's a long walk.

He is unusually short for a man, she sees now, maybe shorter than her. And his hair can be described only as Elvis-style. Perhaps it's this ridiculousness he has gained that makes her go back, slide into the car beside him, tucking her nightgown close around her knees. He does take her home, not saying a word on the way, just smoking with great concentration. He doesn't even peel out when he drops her in the road—he pulls away as smoothly as when he picked her up. She stands there watching until the darkness has sealed over the taillights.

bath

When she comes in the door clicks like a firecracker. Her lightest steps draw excruciating squeaks from the floor planks. She stops and waits. There it is: the gentlest, most content breathing. Even this softest sound tearing open the quiet. She looks in at him. His eyes are sealed tight and he does not appear to have moved. Yet he looks different to her, somehow like someone else's son. He looks alien and full of secrets.

Closing doors behind her to keep the noise from him, she goes into the bathroom and turns on the faucet. The bathwater roars. In one movement, the nightgown is off. Her body is starkly real in the light, real as only flesh is. Her skin thick and clammy with sweat. She hangs the gown on the hook on the door. It hangs in docile folds, as still as a museum piece. She rubs at her bright lips in the mirror. They will have returned to their normal, pale color by morning, maybe sooner. A white foot slaps on white porcelain, a foot snarled with bones. It slides into the hot water. She still has some hours before he is up.

A Familiar White Corridor

Ike's golden tail like a light flicking on and off through the underbrush. It's November and I'm following Ike and Ike's following Ray and I just want to see the fucking discovery and get out of here. Watching for the tail's spontaneous flash because Ray is out of sight though I can hear the heavy rustling passage of his legs not far ahead. Not much of a trail, more like the faded scar of a cowpath, a slight indentation where the limp winter grass is flattened, probably by Ray since Ray's dad hasn't had cattle in years. A pale and cloudless sky filtering through the black branches. Cold, cold even though we're walking fast at the pace set by Ray, who has surged ahead, and shouts back. Shouts all the time. Just like his dad. Talks to you like you're hard of hearing, in a raucous, arrogant voice like his dad's. His dad is an alcoholic with the big gut hanging in his tee shirt and the burning eyes and the sagging yellow face. I can see Ray's future in that face. I can see his eyes, how they'll sink into their sockets and burn and hollow out too someday. In August I saw Ray's dad in the recliner at dawn on a Sunday morning as I was sneaking out so they wouldn't know I'd slept in Ray's room and he stared at me like he was dead and like I was dead, and for a second I thought he was, but then he lifted the beer can from his crotch and sucked on it and I could see he was still alive, but I didn't think he deserved to be. I saw Ray's dad as a corpse then and I've never been able to shake that image, or wanted to. That was in August a week before I left for school and that was when I finally broke up with Ray.

The others are right behind me, breathing hard. Walk a little faster so you can think. I think how this is like the past again, like this summer. My past gives me the creeps now that I've got some distance from it. I can see it too clearly and I see it's weird and enveloping and I remember how it closed around me and changed me. But I have a new past now, in which my schoolmates trudge behind me, through the underbrush wherever I lead. My new friends, bored suburban college brats. I'm like a lab rat for them, and they want some material, and they're getting it, you get it the second you meet Ray. But I'm drawing the line at Ray's dad, there's no way they're meeting him. Everybody says he raped a twelve-year-old girl one time. They started saying this when I was just a kid, and my dad said it was true. My dad told me to stay away from Ray after that, but then my dad died, and I never knew whether to believe him anyway, because how would he know? He was on the booze about as much as Ray's dad. And I grew up, and I became an artist and Ray and I were the only ones who took art that last year they offered it at my high school, so it was just me and Ray and the long carved-up wooden tables in the big garage where the teacher left us alone all the time, and it was around that time that people started saying Ray was crazy, and I liked that.

It's November alright, a day exactly like November, silver air, dying leaves. The woods standing still, too cold for much movement. Our movements are startling and magnified in the quiet; the sharp sounds of twigs snapping and the sounds of the brush scraping our coats and legs. Ike's just ahead. His tail's stopped flickering clear of the brush now, and he's in the clearing, his golden body shaking under the incessant wag. I emerge first into the clearing, I see

Ray's white face and angry eyes, clear and blue like stones in the creek bed.

"Here we are," he says.

"Here we are?" I say.

"This is it," he says.

"What's it?" I say.

"This!" he says, spreading his arms and stepping away from me. I sense the others behind me. I sense them standing there behind their eyes. With their expectation climbing.

There's nothing in the clearing. It's a clearing, it's a vacant space where the trees have been cut back in a horseshoe shape, it's an oval plane of gray winter grass.

Ray's over at one of the stumps motioning to us. He puts his boot up on the stump and rattles something with it. The thing rattles loud and flashes a little in the dull light. We gather in a circle around the stump. The rattling slows and disintegrates and I hear the wind, imperceptible in the woods, moving in the clearing. It's a baking tin. A charred, rectangular baking tin tottering on the stump. "Well?" somebody says.

Ray does not look up. He stares very intently at the stump, the thin line of a smile curling up on his face. His fists are clenched, white. He's excited. He rubs his hands on his thighs. He doesn't wear a coat, just a red tee-shirt and ripped jeans, and it's too cold to be without a coat, very cold and the sun is beginning to set and the wind is picking up.

"This is what I feed him in," Ray says at last, through the curling smile.

"Feed what in?" Britney whispers.

"A biscuit a day for ten days and I'm his best friend. Fucker can't get enough. Bread and butter for the masses, bread and butter for the mammoth! A little cream, a little jam, a little salt-oh-the-earth and a mother-*fuckin'* good biscuit!" He pauses, narrows his eyes. "Bisquick," he snaps. "You schoolbirds know what Bisquick is?"

"What the hell are you talking about Ray?" I say.

"My pet. The woolly mammoth. The *pre-his-toric* kind. The only one left on the entire North American continent," he says, puffing up his chest.

"You dragged us up here for this?" I'm glaring at his clear blue eyes, I'm trying to see into them, I'm forgetting that I never could. Vacant, not clear. There was no Ray. There was nothing inside, nothing locatable.

"The woolly mammoth as pet. Sanitary, gentle, good-tempered. One Bisquick a day, just add piss-water for salt mineral."

"Jesus Christ, Ray." I'm walking off at a normal pace, but with determination. I'm not walking fast because I'm not afraid. Ray's not crazy, he's just an asshole starving for attention. I stop ten feet into the woods and let the others by, proclaiming as they pass, "Don't worry, guys. Ray's not crazy, he's just an asshole starving for attention," loud enough for Ray, standing like a scarecrow on the stump, one foot in the baking tin, to hear.

He plunges off the stump fast as a wolf. He's running at me with his hands out like they're ready to strangle me. I twist away but he catches me, grabbing at my waist and hair. He yanks my head back by the hair, exposing my throat, making my mouth fall open and gasp. My eyes roll back to the treetops, the dimming sky, the eclipse of Ray's face, unshaven, all teeth and chin and hatred. I remember being this close to his face with a different emotion. I claw at the hatred. His grip loosens.

I'm running and the others are running too, ahead of me, so far ahead now I can see only glimpses of their dark heels through the trees. Ike is barking repeatedly not far behind. The trail is dense and slick with long grass. It's hard to see with the black tree trunks blending into the darkness and the trail beginning to blend with the dark brush. Then, pointed elbows moving in a white jacket ahead, one of the girls, Britney. I move alongside her. She's breathing hard, and so am I. But there are no footsteps behind us. We keep walking fast. We don't talk. Her face is hard to see. I see white in her eyes the same shape as the tiny thin fingernail-clipping moon high above. I recognize the sky from my childhood, but so what? That long-gone sky like a stranger caught in a photograph, hiding in the wings.

I keep walking fast beside Britney, just walking and not thinking.

Pretty soon I see red lights flicking on and off through the leaves. Then noise behind us suddenly, fast noise, rustling, breath. Ike flashes past, tail going. Running again, the red taillights of my pickup glowing ahead, the slam of a screen door, the old man's heavy slurry voice shouting. We emerge from the trail. The house is just below, and my pickup is running in the driveway, tailgate down. One of the guys is behind the wheel, I can't tell which, a face in the window, scared, twisted around looking for us. Ray's dad is coming off the porch in a rage, storming onto the sidewalk in his bare feet. Ray's dad is between us and the pickup now, rushing the pickup, slapping his hands repeatedly on the window and on the image of a stricken face behind the glass.

All of this happening so fast as though at once. Ray coming up from behind, suddenly from the trail, so suddenly he almost has me. I'm running at the screen door, pulling Britney by the wrist but the wrist slips away. The old man's in the driveway, still pounding his fist at the pickup's window. I'm in the house, I'm in the familiar white corridor, I remember the big cupboard doors and how they unfold from the walls and swing both ways. Black night through the dots of the screen, but no faces. I pull a door between my body and the screen and it sticks in the narrowness. Yellow light at the other end of the corridor, the end leading into the kitchen, but I pull the next door between it, and the light is squeezed out, and inside it's gray and smothering. A rectangular space like a telephone booth except smaller. I bet I've walked through here a hundred times. I remember this white corridor, spotted with stains and fly-specks. I remember hiding in here before, hide-and-go-seek. I lean my face on the specks, still breathing hard, so tired. I try to slow my breath so I can hear what's going on. Nothing. Not a sound. I wait for a long time, wait until I feel ready to run again. I shape a plan: creep out the house by the door on the other side of the porch, across the shadowed yard full of junk cars and machinery, making the shape of these things with my own form, under the barbed wire and into the field where the old nag is starving and chews at his hooves so long they've curled up so he can hardly walk, through the nag's field and down into the creek bed, then out on the dirt road, five miles to the pavement, beneath that old sky again.

I swing open the door leading into the house at the same time the door behind me swings open, and I jump and turn and face him—Ray's dad, corpse. His eyes sagging and burning, he's all hollowness and gut and stinking of alcohol. I've surprised him but the surprise moves into his eyes too slowly and I see he's long gone drunk. "Lemme by," he says. I move out from the corridor into the yellow light of the kitchen, him coming behind me. I'm trying not to show anything, I'm trying not to shake. It's warm and close in the kitchen, quiet and humming like summer and it stinks bad. I see him behind me in the wall of reflections shining on the windows, he's looking down, picking at his teeth and swaying a little. A miniature black and white spotted dog lies with its head on its paws on the filthy pine table. I don't know this dog. It's a new dog. Everything is familiar but this dog. I put my hand on his head and he looks up and licks his teeth and strains his eyes at me, pain in them. I hear summer again, crickets and flies buzzing, the way a dirty past buzzes and creeps and crawls its sticky feet all over you like a bacteria. I look again for the old man in the reflection and see his back stooping in the open refrigerator door. I slip behind him and outside.

It's very dark. I remember the mercury light over the barn has been burnt out for years. I hear voices in the darkness, first Ray's and then Britney's softer one. Their figures grow from the darkness by the silver bumper of my pickup. Ray's talking loudly and wildly about the woolly mammoth. Britney sounds like she's trying to argue with him. Someone else laughs. The twisted-around heads of the others through the pickup's back window. They sound the horn, once, twice. I move along the porch to the other side of the house, step down into the dirt. A dark passage between the bushes and the house.

The Sensation of Dough

You stand on the veranda of your sister's house long after nightfall. The dishes have been washed by now and are drying inside on the wooden rack, dampening the towel beneath. Supper, long since cold, sits in towel-covered bowls in the cool dark beneath the overhanging cupboard. You knock, there is a rustling inside, and the red curtain in the front window moves, flickering the shadow of your sister's head. You step back to make room on this tiny veranda, which is really just a rectangle cut from the side of the plain, adobe house no different from any of the houses on this road. You look out at the long, moon-illumined road you have come up and turn it, again, over in your mind. What has happened to you today. How near it was, how clear a sign that something is at work for you and something coming to you. You look back at the thick, tightly sealed door, and at last it opens. Yellow, electric light gushes and scatters the moonlight papering the veranda walls. She is there, but before she can open the door any wider, you say, Come out.

She hesitates, or maybe she doesn't. She slips out and pulls the door shut and looks up at you questioningly as the moon settles on her face, and you should speak now, tell her right away, before the rooftops eclipse the moon and hide her face. But she is not your sister yet. Her body appears smaller than you remember, and there is the foreign aroma of children and food on her; she is alien to you, so, you wait.

Instead you talk about how hot the fields were today and how the squash is coming on plaguelike. About your minimum wage, seasonal job that leaves your hands cracked and splintered with the transparent hairs from the bean plants you've picked all day. You don't ask about the family that shifts behind these thick white walls, every now and then uttering muffled words. Not about the husband whose ruddy hands splay like continents at the ends of his arms, nor the boy or girl whose black-eyed, animalish stares leave you squeamish. Even though you know they await her impatiently in the lamplit room—wait without really knowing they are waiting, without being able to name the faint but persistent unease they feel when she is absent—you don't ask. She floats like an uprooted tooth before you, white-bloused, small, bright eyes blinking rabbit-like as you talk. Soon the children will come to the window; maybe you will see a tiny face separate the curtain and wall, and maybe she will twitch, lean on one hip and then the other, nod too quickly in response, giving away that the night is too big for her, the moon too long and fat and wild for her whose eyes and ears have grown so small. Perhaps you will see that your sister is no longer up to nights like this one, summer nights in full bloom. Already it seems she is edging away inconspicuously, inch by inch out from the door to a position that will allow her to see the window. She tucks her arms behind her back, leans back on her arms on the wall and pooches her abdomen out. It bulges like a melon between you. How can you speak now?

Or maybe you are misreading her. There are so many possibilities . . . Maybe it is instead that the huge night tempts her, and it is this that makes her rein her eyes in when they stray off the veranda and that pulls with its precautionary thread her face again and again toward the window. Perhaps she envies you your walking in it; she can see how all down the moon-white road leading to her house you've walked drenched in this night. You must reek of it, of moonlight as she reeks of children and food. Could it be that considering you, standing there blinking at you in your earth-smeared clothes and skin, the clean, sweet smell of dirt on you, it occurs to her that she hates the thought of the dishes drying inside on the rack, hates the way each puddle of water slowly, agonizingly desiccates, shrinking increment by increment the way the secondhand shows the shrinking and shriveling away of her life second by second? And her husband—you remember how he plunked his stony heels on the boy's bare back as the boy lay on the floor before his chair, an action surely intended as fatherly, but the scaliness of those heels and the tiny bits of skin that flaked, white and dead, onto the boy's back; they turned your stomach. And the daughter continually causing that startling movement at the curtains—could it be that it occurs to your sister now, tonight for the first time, that none of these are a part of her real life, her inner life of desire?

But knowing that sometimes, even between sisters, smalltalk is necessary as a bridge to some older, simpler intimacy, you continue to kill time with your chatter. Then suddenly among these clattering words, she reaches and takes your wrists. She cups your hands palm up in her palms, scrutinizes them, then straightens the fingers one by one where they curl naturally and examines these. She turns your hands over and looks carefully at the backs, then the fingernails. You know your own hands, but looking at them with her and beneath them her softer, pinkish ones, how exotic and complicated they appear, with their dark tanned skin puckered around the knuckles, the joints rowed like tiny cabbages, the fresh scabs and palish scars, the ragged nails rimmed with black dirt. All day these hands have buried seeds on the farm where you have worked since you came to your sister's town at the beginning of spring. All day they smoothed the holes over, patted them and moved on.

Your sister asks, Don't you want to come in and wash up?

You do not.

On the day something finally happened to you, you saw the red curtain that marks your sister's house apart from the others as you approached from the road. You saw the moon in the veranda, papering its rough adobe cool silver. The doorknob and the brass lock too glowed so strongly you could see them from the road. It was then, it seems, you decided you would not go inside tonight. Why would you leave all this light, all this bigness, for the electric light of her stale, orderly living room? Tonight, you decided, you had no desire to enter the close, animalish smell of a family, of bodies that somehow had all acquired the same smell. You looked up at the sky then, and felt young as you stepped onto your sister's veranda. You had come to tell her what had happened to you today. You felt young thinking of what you had to tell her, this sister with the family that would gird her when she opened the door, their faces crescenting her, peeking out to see who was there, but she would step out right away onto the veranda, knowing instantly with a sister's intuition that something—something good—had finally happened to you. Like when she claimed to have felt the roots of her own hair itching as you were cutting yours off in another country. Or when, this spring, only days before you returned to this town whose noon pavement nearly burns holes in the soles of your sandals, she felt, she said, so cold she could not leave her bed; she lay dreaming of snow while your train plowed through drifts on its way south, to her, after so many years.

You had not yet knocked. You saw a portion of the kitchen in the strip between the curtain and the window. You saw the dishes drying in the wooden rack and the bowls under the cupboard in the cool dark. You could almost smell the food under the white cloths. You saw just the edge of the dough rolled out on the pine cutting board like a section of skin, but you knew this dough, you knew the shape your sister made it in and you could almost feel it, dry and moist, firm and supple at once, something like a young girl's skin, something like the daughter's, your niece's, skin must feel fresh out of the bath, dusted with powder. When you were a girl your hands knew the touch of dough often—yours and your sister's too, for it was your job together to make the family's bread, three loaves a week. How sick you got of that clammy touch, that melty shapelessness. Now, your fingers ache with the remembrance of the sensation of dough.

But your sister did not step out right away, nor did she ask you inside even though you had decided you would not come inside tonight, and now—now, when the moon's swath has shifted so that only you are illuminated, she left in shadow, is the time to speak to her. The moon is urging you to speak. It spotlights your half of the veranda like a stage, spotlights you on it. But you carry your news like a stone concealed in your pocket, and you have carried it there since it happened this afternoon, fumbling with it, rolling it back and forth and over and over in the clammy grip of your mind. You begin to wonder if this wear and tear the stone has undergone may have changed it. This fixation, this concentrated gazing on it giving it perhaps more significance than in reality it had. You know the dangers of speaking it aloud. It is tempting to leave this stone in its pocket.

There is also the possibility that when you reveal your news, your sister will blink spastically like she does when she's nervous, she will look out at the sky embarrassed—of you, embarrassed of your descriptions, your silly details and fantasies and your endless lack of lovers—and when she turns back she will be smiling, but too widely with lips tight, and tonight as her husband scratches his raspy feet on the bedrails in his half-sleep, she will pray with refreshed passion that same tired prayer for you: *Father, send her a husband.*

Then without warning, the door opens and the daughter is there. She lingers between the door and frame, one foot standing on the other. Suddenly brave, she stretches her arms out; she wants picked up. Why should your sister turn her away? She bends down and lifts her onto her hip and becomes suddenly biblical, mother with child.

What do you want? your sister says, inclining her head to touch her nose to the daughter's.

Nothing. The daughter is shy in front of you even though you have visited before. She shrugs and toys with a loose button on your sister's blouse.

What's daddy doing?

Sleeping.

In the chair? Your sister rolls her eyes at you.

The daughter nods and adds, He fell asleep when Juan was rubbing his toes.

And what's Juan doing now?

Reading.

Your sister laughs. You mean pretending to read? She looks at you. He can't yet, but he'll stare at a book for hours just to impress us. Right? She shakes the miniature body on her hip.

He can't really read, the daughter informs you, and pokes her thumb in her mouth. The moon shines for a second on the wet red of her outturned lip before your sister snatches her hand away.

Why do you do that? she says, leaning back to meet her child's eyes. You're too old for that. Do you want people to think you're a baby?

The daughter shakes her head and stares at her thumb. Of course not. Who wants to be thought a baby? The vow is made: she'll stop because she wants to be treated like a grown-up and because her mother has asked her to. When they speak this way—like lovers, forehead on forehead, eyelash brushing eyelash—you feel you should turn your head.

When the daughter has gone back in, armed with tasks; teeth to be brushed, pajamas climbed into, your sister looks down at her sandaled feet, or at yours. You know what she is thinking. She is thinking about the dough drying on the board like a body. Soon it will be too late to form the dough. The dough will keep until tomorrow, but the loaf it produces will be slightly dry. It would be best to make the loaf tonight.

She crosses her arms over her belly, which is pooched out again. She yawns.

I'm going in, she says, holding you away from her by the shoulders so she can see your face. You can feel the warmth and the softness of her hands through your cotton sleeves. And maybe this simple touch is all you needed.

But walking home to your unlit windows, you can't help thinking, does it not occur to her any more that something might still happen to you? She might have sensed it. She might not have given up completely on you yet. Because, after all, something did happen today, something significant. Anyone would think so. The late afternoon rain had let you off work early and you had walked in from the farm and were headed downtown, just wandering. The white adobes facing the street sat lined in strings of raindrops. Your sandals were wet and your heels squeaked on the leather with each step. The straw field hat hung by its string down your back. With it and your dark, rain-damp hair you must have looked like a girl from a village, old-worldish and young, a girl who should have been wearing a sundress instead of work pants. You were crossing the square, your sandals squeaking and squeaking. The heat was regathering itself after the rain and people were leaning in their windows trying to decide if it would get hot enough again to continue napping as they had napped through the rain. Most had already decided it would and pulled their shutters closed. Some were surely already asleep, and you could almost hear their breaths rising and falling, lengthening and deepening behind the walls, and it was this you were listening for when the pale-eyed man, beautiful man with a tiger's walk, who you had passed before on the sidewalk and who had seemed to notice you then, too, put his head in the window, saw you, and almost spoke.

What My Father Taught Me

The next thing my father taught me was how not to be afraid of the dark. He came to me with this proposition like a businessman. He said if I could learn not to fear the dark I could learn not to fear anything. He set everything out very clearly so I would know exactly what I was getting into. He showed me the cistern in the broad daylight. I put my bare feet at the edge of the hole and gripped it with my toes and leaned to look in. The concrete was almost too hot to stand on and the edge was scabby. The cistern was dry and it had been for years. The sun shone light inside but it didn't reach the bottom. The bottom lay in dim gray. But it didn't look too dirty and no cobwebs and I could feel a little cool stretch up from it. The sky spread out outside the hole, so pale pale blue it was like no color at all. My father squatted beside me. He smelled like beer. He ran his fingers the bumpy round of the hole. They were a roughnecker's fingers, thick and strong and black oil in their creases. I kept one hand on his blue-jeaned knee as I leaned to look down in. Once we kept hearing a cat meow and meow and meow, turned out it had fallen down in the cistern. My father got a ladder and brought it out. At first I thought it was alive, just really skinny and tired, but it was dead. Its body gone hard and eyes like bottle glass. The cistern was deep, about fifteen feet said my father. He asked me what I saw in the hole and I said nothing. He said that's right, nothing there.

He stood and slid the wooden lid over the hole with his boot. Then he lifted the concrete block that held the lid down and put it on the lid. He stepped back and crossed his arms on his chest. I could feel him looking at me but I kept looking at the block on the lid. At his boots half on the lid and half on the concrete. They were set a little apart, John Wayne style. His jeans were tucked in to keep them from dragging in the mud. The leather was worn near white on the points of his boots and on the heels were black spur marks. I knew he was waiting for me to say if we had a deal but I just stood there looking down. He said nobody's going to make you. He waited a little bit more then he sort of grunted and said you can't teach somebody something they don't want to learn, animals or people, don't matter, and then he walked off. I was still staring at the concrete where his boots had been. The sun was lighting up the thousands of different-shaped pieces of stones in it and thousands of colors, red, blue, gold. I closed my eyes and I could still see those stones, a mesh of silvery patterns on the fire-color back of my eyelids. With all that sight in me, I thought, with all that sight why should I be afraid of the dark?

I opened my eyes and looked for my father. The silvery patterns were jumping like snakes in the air. I saw both halves of the barn door were open. As I walked out there the silvery snakes dissolved in the white air. I found my father behind the wall of hay stacked ceiling-high. I told him okay. I said I'll do it but he just kept pulling bales down. He had a pair of wire cutters in his hand and he ran his thumb under the baling wire and lifted it tight like an upside-down telephone line. He clipped it at the top and the hay fell apart. He didn't look at me or say anything, he just kept pulling bales down and cutting them open.

After supper my father told me to go to my room and get my sleeping bag. I knew what was going to happen so before I came down I went in his room that used to be the spare room and got in the drawer of my mother's old things.

The drawer still smelled like her, like stale roses. My fingers found the rosary where they last hid it, in the yellowing finger of one of her felt wedding gloves. He didn't know I saved the rosary but I didn't think he ever looked in there. I didn't know any of the rosary prayers but you don't have to for them to work and I liked the smooth feel of the wooden beads and their kernel shape between my fingers. I knelt at the top of the stairs where the full moon was in the window at the end of the hall, a perfect round construction paper yellow in the top pane. I could still see the circle of its glow as I prayed, eyes closed, pressing those beads. In the middle of the prayer I fell into wishing a little bit she was still alive but I didn't go too far down that road. I thought about slipping it in my skirt pocket, taking it with me into the cistern, then changed my mind. I hid it under the blankets in the linen closet. I didn't need it. I wasn't afraid. He was calling me. I had to get downstairs.

My mother died a horrible death. She was parked alongside the road with the hood up, car overheated we guess. She was leaning in the hood. Some guy pulled over to help and parked his pickup in front of her, his tail-end pretty close to her car. Somebody on the highway went to sleep or was drunk or something and came along and hit the back of her car, ramming it into the other guy's bumper and chopping my mother in two pieces.

My father was away in the army when this happened. When he came back he spent two weeks in that room that used to be their bedroom not leaving it once. One day he opened the door and told me to come in there. He told me to get some things of hers I wanted. She didn't have much. I got a brooch shaped like a cat with little topaz slivers for the eyes and her wedding gloves and I hid the rosary in one finger. He kept her wedding ring and some scarves and a half-used bottle of perfume and a piece of her hair. These we put in the bottom drawer of the dresser in the spare room, the room my father sleeps in now. They didn't even fill it up. The rest, he said, was for throwing out. Even the little pocket bible and the crucifix and the prayer cloth she used to kneel on and pray. He never could stand, he said, her religious streak. We piled it all in the oil drums back of the house and burnt it. All her clothes and everything. The sleeves of her dresses hung over the rust-chewed sides, the chunks of her high heels poked out the holes. My father didn't go back to the army. He stayed home, to take over my education, as he put it. And he didn't bring her up again.

When I came into the kitchen he was putting sandwiches in my lunchbox. I showed him the sleeping bag and pillow. He felt the bag as if making sure it was there then he stared at the pillow. I was holding it up long so it covered almost all of me clear to my chin. He yanked at the bottom of it and I gripped it tighter. I thought he was going to take my pillow. He shook his head and grinned like I was the stupidest thing he'd ever seen. Then he jerked on the pillowcase and slipped it off and held it up in two fingers. No need to dirty this too he said.

He told me to get anything else I wanted so I went out to the fridge on the back porch where we kept the six-packs of pop and got two bottles of strawberry. The pop was stacked on a half-gone case of beer. I thought about taking one, I don't know why. He really wouldn't have liked that. I'd never tasted a beer before. It was Coors. It was pee yellow and taller and skinnier than regular cans. I put it back. When I came back in the house I gave him the bottles of pop and he put one in my lunchbox and left one on the counter. I guessed he didn't think I needed two. I didn't ask, with him I didn't ask questions. But I wasn't afraid of him. He was my father.

When he was done filling his canteen from the tap he screwed the cap on and looped the cap-chain over my finger. I was holding my sleeping bag and pillow and he put my lunchbox on top of these and I added the canteen. Then he put both hands on my shoulders and guided me to the back door. He stopped at the closet and pulled his big army jacket off a metal hanger. He held it out in front of me by the shoulders. It was so huge and so stiff it looked like someone was inside it, some dead soldier. You won't be scared in this he said. This has been a lot scarier places than down there. He made me step inside it.

Outside the dark was bigger than ever, the moon hidden behind the roof. No wind at all, so still I could hear the horses chewing in the barn. The cistern was right out the back door, the concrete block still holding down the lid as if waiting for me. My father looked at me and said well are you going to do this yourself or not?

I couldn't lift the block so I put my fingers in it and dragged it off the lid. I said we don't need this. That lid won't move anyhow, no wind tonight. My father was staring at the lid and I didn't know if he heard me. I pushed the block off the cistern's platform. The old doghouse was right there so I rolled it in there and let it fall in the dished-out place in the straw where Sam used to lay before the coyotes got him. I thought it might be better down in there without that block over the lid. That block was awful heavy.

When I stood up my father was looking at me, it was like he had spaced off a little while. He did that a lot. He said what are you doing? I was standing in the shadow of the doghouse and I didn't think he could see my face. He was standing in the reach of the back door light and I could see his face clear enough but there was nothing in it I could read. It was as blank as ever. Nothing I said and he looked back down at his boots.

I kicked the wooden lid off with my boot. The hole was really dark now. All you could see in it was a foggy gray reflection from the mercury light, you couldn't see the bottom so it looked like there was no bottom, like it went on forever and ever. We squatted and leaned over the hole together and my father switched on his flashlight and poked it inside. I kept one hand on his blue-jeaned knee and leaned on in and saw how the dark opened when the yellowish stick of light poked it and I saw what, really, I knew—the cistern did have a bottom, it was only concrete and nothing else down in that dark. Maybe a little water, trickled in through the cracks.

My father helped me throw the gear in, some things of his and some of mine. I put the canteen and lunchbox in the sleeping bag and lowered it in as far as I could before I dropped it. I heard the canteen and lunchbox thump on the bottom. It was a long way down. I hoped the pop bottle hadn't broken. The pillow drifted down. I stood up and faced him. He was squatting and looking past me out at the barn or somewhere. I put my arms out. He stepped over the hole and braced himself with a boot on its edge, put his hands in my armpits and swung me over the dark. I felt the air open beneath my feet, rising up cool. He lowered me into that cool, sliding his grip down my arms to my hands. When his hands were grasping mine still my feet felt only air and I didn't know how far down it still was. He said I'm letting go. Bend your knees when you land. He let go and the bottom came fast, solid even through the sleeping bag.

I arranged the gear to make things comfortable while my father shone the flashlight down. I wanted him to shine it in the round corners, just in case of spiders, but I wasn't going to ask. Okay I said when I had things the way I wanted them. The bare pillow was propped against the wall, the sleeping bag out smooth and the lunchbox and canteen where I could find them. Ready? he said. Yeah I said. You done saw there was nothing down there, did'n you? I looked up but all I could see was the fuzzy glare of the flashlight. Yeah I said into it. He said Nothing to be a-feared of. You sleep tight. I'll see you in the morning. I said okay and my voice was really small. The flashlight moved out of the hole. I saw the TV antenna on top of the roof branch like a stick man and beyond that some stars on the black sky before I saw the lid come over the hole, making the dark in the cistern one solid whole. I sat down. It was cool at the bottom of the cistern, almost cold. I pulled the sleeping bag up around my shoulders. It was probably going to get cold. My eyes were staring hard trying to see something but they couldn't see anything but black. I closed them and tried to see something on the back of my eyelids but there was nothing there. There were things I could do. I could have the bottle of pop. I could think about getting my own horse. I could call for my father.

I wondered if he had left. I didn't hear him. Then I heard the concrete block drop on the lid, sealing it good. He had found it. Then the scrape of his bootsteps fading as he left. I closed my eyes and saw him going inside where all the lights were on. I saw him sitting down at the kitchen table and staring into all that light but him not seeing anything more than I was. That must be how it was to be him. I got

74

in the sleeping bag and burrowed down in the pillow. That was better. It was warm now and quiet and very dark in that hole and I didn't see any reason to want out.

Broken Coin *

I saw him out to the road. I walked him down the long driveway that ran from the farmhouse to the road. The sun was not yet up and the gravel driveway was silver and the air bluish and rustling with lingering night ghosts. In the dim I could just make out the prongs of his hands at the ends of his swinging arms as he walked ahead. He wanted to get an early start. He wanted to get as far as he could before the scorching July heat set in. Then he would find a shady spot, wait the day out, resting, saving up his strength to move again at night, all night. This was his way—it was, he told me, the way of the nomad. I understood this. I got out of bed before him, and I didn't insist he stay for breakfast.

His pack was full on his back but he walked easily in his lunging, tigerly stride. He stopped when he reached the road. He stopped before stepping into its current and looked back for me and I came up beside him. The road ran before us, a river of white limestone glowing in the dark-

*Fractus Tessera: A symbol from medieval alchemy, the coin two friends break and share upon parting ways.

ness. We stood together on its bank and it seemed I was going with him.

The arms of the road spread north and south like a cross and at both ends clove hills we couldn't see beyond. Lucas squinted past the southern hill, at what he knew was there: seas of waist-high prairie speckled with cattle, collapsing homesteads like mine, with their rotting barns and silos, lines and lines of barbed wire and telephone wire and telephone poles, repeating and repeating, and above it all, the boundless, tundral sky. Lucas did not look both ways. He looked south, his focus was on his way. I looked north, and saw him top the white hill there as he had day before yesterday, an omen, a mirage emerging from the dust, shimmery and see-through with the sun all on him, then denser, then flesh, blood, then a man, a man I loved—Lucas, back after so long and I couldn't believe it.

But now the sun was coming up behind us. Fast. Nothing was stopping it. Some light was leaking through the crack it made in the horizon and throwing our shadows thinly on the road. That was the way of Lucas and I and it was okay. I waited, he wandered. He sought out there, I sought in here, this I understood. Then one day he would reappear, materializing from the white light of years of absence. I looked at our shadows. We were two pointed ghosts, daggers standing side by side.

I looped my arms around him and put my face in his neck. The neck was damp, the smell of his sweat just under the skin.

Into his ear, I said, Thanks for coming.

When I stepped back he was smiling. He said, I'll always come.

I know.

He dug in his jeans pocket. When his hand came out there was something in it, between his thumb and forefinger something small and sharp the sun twisted off.

Suddenly from behind we heard the sounds of steps crunching the gravel. I turned and saw two figures coming up the dip in the road from the north. They were covered head to toe in black robes and black shawls drawn close over their heads. The top halves of their faces were covered too and you couldn't see their eyes, I didn't know how they could see or if they could. They struggled up the hill, leaning into the incline. One held a bundle wrapped tightly in the same black cloth. They shuffled up close—they were moving at a turtle's pace—too close and at first we thought they were going to walk right through us. But they stopped and we stepped back from the road to open up some space. They were panting and their breath was sour in our faces. They were old—what little skin we could see was withered and sagged past their jawbones and the dry lines of their lips were spoked by tiny wrinkles. On the black bundle, the one's hands were blue, and maps of veins showed through the tissue paper skin. As I studied the bundle, I thought I saw a twitch at its rounded end—a living jerk deep within the wraps of cloth.

What hills, spoke one. The voice was female, high and papery. What a death in those hills.

We didn't expect a death in those hills, but we got one, said the other, in a voice deeper and scratchier, though also female. She added informatively, We buried it in the ditch. You don't want to get far off the road.

There are bogs in the pastures.

We dug a grave with strong branches. You don't have to make them deep for the little things.

It was just a little death, said the first one, a coated, yellowish tongue poking between the lips like a piece of wood.

And before that, we had another one. That was in the mountains.

Yes, said the other. That was in the mountains.

Far from here.

Not particularly far.

No, not that far. That one we buried in the stream.

The stream took it. Not like the one before that. That one everything was frozen. We couldn't bury that one at all.

We had to leave it.

We left it in the frozen road.

Someone would come along.

Someone has come along by now.

They looked at each other, or the bound heads rotated as if their eyes could see through the visors of cloth and I wondered if they could, if they had laser eyes or eyes with x-ray abilities. They added in unison, Just as you two have come along now.

Lucas and I looked at each other.

What a run of bad luck.

The other nodded. What a run.

The one holding the bundle looked down at it. She said—and I thought I detected sadness in her until now cheerful voice—This is the last one left.

As we watched she unpeeled the layers of black cotton, lifting layer after layer as one lifts away the moldy leaves of a cabbage. At last we saw skin—a tiny fleshy arm. She lifted a final layer and a baby's red, turnipish face appeared.

We're taking it to be baptized, she said, sealing the cloth back over its mouth. If it survives.

We gave them directions to the spring—Lucas gave them directions, I had never been myself. The spring was nearby, and I could have found it on my own. There really was no excuse for not having visited it yet. The spring was a place of magic, it could save you. There really was no excuse. How much longer would I wait in the old farmhouse, reading decades in the leaves of wallpaper that curled from the molded walls like an old midwife reads tea leaves?

The spring lay in the limestone-studded hills to the southwest. The Virgin was said to have appeared there, touched her divine feet to the waters, and imparted healing powers to them. People from all over the countryside used to come and camp in the pastures around it. They heard whispers, they saw visions in the cottonwood treetops. Years ago, Lucas had told me just last night, he had seen a boy healed there. The boy was near suffocating with pneumonia. Each choked breath he spit stones of yellow phlegm onto the grass. The healer held him in the water so long Lucas thought he would have drowned but the boy came up shining, face haloed with light and the coughing was gone. Over that night's campfire the boy told how the choice came to him in the image of two doorways. Through one he saw fire and through the other ice. He chose fire.

The two of them repeated Lucas's directions and moved on without thanking him, their feet in the gravel rasping the dawn quiet. As their stooped black figures topped the first hill to the south, I said to Lucas, How can it breathe? He didn't know.

Now the sun had risen enough there was a gap between it and the earth. The sun was a perfect circle, its light still soft enough its clean edges could be seen. Neither was the heat bad yet, but it was there, a force waiting beneath the dawn.

You should go, I said to him.

He nodded and shifted under his pack to face me.

I want to—he paused, seemed at a loss. He held his hand up between us as he had started to before. The thumb and forefinger were pressing a band of light. He tried again: There's this—

A hawk called and swung very low over us. It arced to light on a fencepost not twenty feet away. We looked up at the sky it had appeared in, a sky the color of smoke. Somewhere in its depths we heard a faint crescendoing, an engine. We watched and listened until an airplane poked through. It was coming straight at us. It too was flying very low, like a crop sprayer but it was not a crop sprayer. It buzzed over our heads and spiraled back up into the sky. The hawk called again. It blinked at us and lifted and lowered its wings, lifted and lowered its wings. What is the world trying to tell us? I thought. Something. Together we took a deep breath.

This—Lucas began again, and twisted his wrist to hold it up in the fresh sunlight, where it gave a bigger shine.

As the shine spilled out, touching my face, the sound of another engine, on the road this time, cut the air. A jeep popped over the north hill. A military jeep, its top off, painted camouflage. It pulled up and stopped, tires grinding, before us. There were two soldiers in it wearing army fatigues and caps that shaded their eyes. The driver said, We're looking for two old women. They're dressed in black, like nuns—

I cut him off. They went over that hill, I said, pointing a long arm south. And not long ago.

He nodded, pounded the gas and the jeep drove off, spinning dust in our mouths.

By this time the young sun had bleached the road as white as the cattle bones scattered in the fields. The grass in the ditches, too, had been scorched colorless over the droughted summer, not a hint of green remained in it. Looking south I saw the future. I saw Lucas's shape disappearing over that hill into this paleness. I saw his feet going over and over on the road, one replacing the other, lifting and dropping and lifting and dropping in an endless recycling of feet. I dropped my head on his shoulder and leaned into him. His body did not sway. He was solid, a pillar. His arms came around me and there was no longer any time left.

We heard the shuffling. The same shuffling, already very close. The rhythmic back and forth of their feet scraping the gravel and between this the softer rhythm of their heavy skirts dragging in the dirt. Keeping my head on his arm I looked down and back through my feet and I saw the skirts come into view, a good three inches of white chalky dust hemming their bottoms. Lucas took his arms away and we faced them together. They had no sense of the polite distance from which to stand. We backed away, but they edged closer yet. Their rancid old-woman smells turned my stomach.

We lost the way, they said at once. They had come from the south, I was sure of it. We had seen them disappear over the south hill with our own eyes, then after them the jeep. Why hadn't the men in the jeep caught them? I looked for the baby, but couldn't distinguish a bundle in all that black cloth.

Where's the baby? Lucas said.

Right here, one responded cheerfully. She patted a tumorous bulge in the region of her liver. I couldn't tell if this was the same one that had carried the baby before. While one jagged jawbone may have been broader than another, or one set of teeth grayer and more crumbled than another, the differences were too slight to recall.

Is it alive? he said, voicing my thoughts.

Of course. It's feeding. We listened for it—the suck suck suck. Our faces must have shown our concern, for her fingers peeled back the layers of cloth to reveal the little pale lips at a wilted breast. What portion of the young cheek I could see was the color of a chili, and glistened with sweat. The sun had started to beat down. It really had.

Isn't it hot? I said.

It is, the one without the baby agreed. What heat. We're sweating rivers.

July. Typical for July, said the other.

Typical for these parts.

Yes, for these parts.

I mean isn't the baby hot? I said, losing patience. Smothered in all that cloth.

Keeps it from the sun. Her vaporous hand patted the bundle.

Best to keep it from the sun. To outwit sunburn.

The one who had not said this giggled. To outwit sunburn, that's right, she said, as if getting a kick out of her companion's words.

Now tell us again. Which way to the spring?

Lucas told them again, this time in greater detail. He pointed firmly to the south: it wasn't far, a mile at best, then half a mile west on a pasture road likely to be grown over, you have to look close for the washed-out ruts—pilgrims to the spring are almost always walkers rather than drivers— follow this road until it fades out, then look for a trail leading southwest a few hundred yards over the high bank that slopes down to the spring. You will know it when you come to it—in a horseshoe of scrawny elm trees and sandplum bushes, the spring breaks from the cracked earth to spill into a little sapphire pool. It's small, its diameter hardly the length between fenceposts. But you'll feel it before you see it, the spring gives off a feeling of calm, it's a jewel in these barren pastures to be sure. There's a spiritual feeling there, just as the legends claim. The water is so clear its surface looks silver, and it tastes strangely sweet and when you let it run through your fingers it trickles down in crystals. He described it so beautifully, his face seemed to take on some of that beauty as he spoke. The blue in his eyes the hue of the water he described, the gray in them its depths. He went on and on, until the thought came that I couldn't bear him to leave, not this time, not again, and then he went on some more and another thought came. It was his thought, I heard it in my head, which was something Lucas and I could sometimes do. In this thought he told me he was stalling for the jeep.

At last they interrupted: That will do, they said, that's enough, making no effort to hide their irritation.

Then: We won't be back.

We won't see you again.

You won't see us again.

We're on our way.

We're off, and they shuffled away, a wriggling pair as if joined at the hip beneath their shawls, over the south hill.

While he was talking Lucas had taken his pack off and set it in the driveway. Now he hoisted it up. He gazed up at the sun, then south.

I really have to be off, he said, regret in his voice.

I nodded.

I'll meet the jeep, he said. It'll be coming back and I'll meet it. It can't miss them this time.

I grabbed his hand and unfolded the fingers. A gold coin lay there like a miniature sun in the hollow of his palm. I took it.

Where did you get it? I said.

The grin I loved opened. In a land faraway.

I grinned back.

Really, he said. It won't be so long this time. Winter. I'll be back before winter.

This was what he had told me last night, too, when he held me in the windowpane, the full moon over our touching faces. Then I had felt bitter when he made this promise, now that sharp feeling was gone. I knew he wanted to keep his word, even if he could not bring his wandering feet to do so.

He held his hand out for the coin and I gave it to him. He pressed it between his thumb and forefinger then held it out flat, parallel to the earth. He nodded for me to take hold of it with him.

I heard an engine, and the rattly sound of tires on gravel, and then I saw the jeep top the southern hill. Lucas dropped his hand. We turned to watch it pull up before us.

Before the soldiers could speak, I said, How could you miss them? They were just here.

The passenger side soldier shook his head. They weren't. We scoured the ditches too. We got out and raked through the ditch grass. They were nowhere.

It sounded weird. *They were nowhere.*

Didn't you try the pastures? I said. The pastures have bogs they could hide in.

The driver looked at me sharply. How do you know the pastures have bogs?

What do you mean?

How well do you know those two?

Lucas straightened his arm protectively across my body.

Don't be ridiculous! I shouted. I told you where to find them, and you screwed it up! For the love of God, they've got a baby.

I felt Lucas's hand rest on the back of my neck.

I grew up here. I know the pastures, he told them.

We looked! they protested together.

We got out and raked through the ditches, said the driver.

We ran our binoculars over the pastures, said the passenger.

They're super strength, said the driver. Suddenly I saw how young he was, only a boy. His face smooth and fleshy. Eagerly he added, They're binoculars to be used in combat.

As are these, said the passenger soldier, reaching into the back. He pulled out two machine guns, propped them between their seats. Uzis, massive and sinister. He added, Not that we've needed them yet. But if we do—

We drove all the way to the other end, interrupted the driver.

The other end. I didn't know where that was. I had never been that far, I didn't think Lucas had either. I slammed my fist on the hood.

Go! I said, pointing to the horizon. We're losing time. They have to be over that hill.

They blinked and looked at Lucas. He gave a curt nod. The soldiers slammed the jeep into gear, spun around in the road and sped off, kicking up that smothering gas of white dust. We covered our mouths.

The sun was bright, the heat gaining strength.

Lucas! I said. I clung to his shirt. Where are they? Why don't they find them?

He slid his hand up and down on my back, caressing. It's okay. It's okay. Maybe they're not all bad. They don't seem to want to kill it.

The hawk that had perched atop the fencepost called. It was still there, watching us all this time. I turned on it. I flapped my arms and ran at it. It rose gracefully from the post, then dipped and swooped at me, wings spread wide. Its curled talons just cleared my head, then it soared into the white sky. I sank to my knees, my face in my hands, tears threatening.

You can't leave now, I breathed into my palms. You can't leave, you can't leave me alone with them.

He came and stood over me in the ditch. I stared at his boots. He said, The day grows older.

The phrase sounded medieval, it sounded absurd, juvenile. I felt anger flare up. My hands fell on his boot tops. The toes were tipped in half-moons of white dust, like the hems of their skirts. How did this happen? I snapped.

What?

You haven't stepped into the road yet. How did your boots get white?

What are you talking about?

Are you in cahoots with them? Is that what's going on?

He spoke my name. Softly, with a tinge of sadness. I rose up and met his eyes. I was looking in them for something I didn't recognize when over his shoulder I saw them coming. Two humped figures approaching slowly, slowly cresting the hill where we stood.

Here they are, I whispered. Grab them! Don't let them go.

Lucas and I turned and they shuffled up close close as was their way. Their breath flooded out in a wave of sourness. The tumor, the baby, was there beneath the breasts.

Here we are.

Here we are, they echoed with glee.

We've had more trouble.

We didn't expect it. They shook their heads at each other.

The run we thought was broken.

The run of bad luck.

We should have known.

Bad luck.

I felt my face go cold, in that brutal heat a cold washed up from deep inside me as she dug in the black depths beneath her breasts. At last she produced the bundle, snugly sealed, a lump of black showing no gaps where the cloth had been wound. She shoved it at my chest. My arms moved to take its stony weight. It was stiff already, hard as a slab of flint.

You bury it, she said. You know these parts better than we, and we've got to get back.

July's bad, but August is worse.

Better to outwit August.

We'd never make it in such heat.

We never would.

They began to shuffle away. Lucas touched the arm of the one nearest him. She stopped, turned her faceless face to him. She didn't say a word. The black panel where eyes should have been. I saw his fingers tighten a little around her elbow.

I think you should wait, he said, not unkindly. Wait a little while.

Wait for what? they said in unison.

Lucas changed strategy. Help us bury it. Don't you want to be part of the burial?

We know how it goes, said one.

We've buried our share, the other.

One by one, her bony blue fingers uncurled Lucas's strong brown ones, one by one, finger by finger, in no hurry, no hurry at all. She picked up his hand and gave it back to him. The pair turned and moved off as one.

Goodbye! they waved back without turning round.

Good burying!

We stood watching them go. From the very same spot we had been standing at since dawn, we stood watching their swaying skirts lick the road around their heels until they vanished over the northern hill. We just stood there, holding our separate things: me a dead baby, and Lucas a golden coin.

They had not been gone long when we heard the buzz of the jeep crescendoing from the south. With my arms full of that awful weight, I sent Lucas my thought. We lunged for the ditch.

As luck would have it, a culvert ran under the driveway where it branched off the road. Weeds had grown over its entrance, tall ruby-stemmed stinkweed and sticky white-spattered milkweed. I shoved the baby through them inside the corrugated pipe. There was no water standing in it thanks to the drought. I crawled in after, just fitting. Lucas would not fit, the pipe was too small. I looked down my prone body and saw him squat and curl his head into his knees. He spread the weeds over his head moments before the jeep pulled up.

We listened to it idle. Then shut off. We heard its rusty doors squeak open, their boots hit the gravel. We heard one say, What did I tell you? Then nothing. We held our breath like the poor dead baby except it would hold its forever. I felt sure they had seen Lucas's head in the weeds and were aiming the uzis at it at that moment. The moment passed. The doors slammed. The jeep pulled away, the hum of its engine dying off to the north, and two of three of us breathed again.

When I had slid out of the culvert and pulled the baby out and laid it in the weeds, Lucas said, What should we do with it?

I said, We have to bury it.

I know that, he said, but I wasn't sure I believed him. I mean where?

He was standing up on the road looking over the pastures. I was kneeling over the baby. Tears blurring my gaze.

Poor thing, I whispered. Poor little thing.

The words seemed absurd since there was nothing to indicate it was a baby. It was a black oval lump of cloth. Inside could have been a loaf of bread gone hard and weighted with stones, or a big rock they picked up from the side of the road. They could have replaced it with anything. Lucas came and knelt beside me. His arm came over my shoulders and he pulled me into him. Together we looked down at it. He put his large brown hand on the lump. His fingers curled a moment as if not sure what to do. Then they began to search the cloth. They found an end and lifted. They peeled the layers away, as the old women had before. The curve of a head began to emerge. The petite prongs of white fingers, the transparent chips of tiny fingernails. He lifted the final layer and there was the face. So red before, it was now as white as the road. The blood already stilled under the skin. Yet for an instant I thought I saw its eyelids twitch. For an instant I thought we should feel for a pulse. Hearing my thought, Lucas put two fingers on the miniature throat. But shortly he took them up. We looked at it dead there together, holding each other, and it seemed to me our own.

The spring, I said softly.

Lucas breathed out. He laid the cloth over the face and stood abruptly. I felt a cold, like a wound, open on my side where his body had been next to mine.

It's too far, he said, standing over me. It's too far and too hot.

Maybe it would—

No.

How do you know?

I know.

How?

Because I made it up.

The fire and the ice?

No. That part was true. But the next day the boy died. The healing didn't work. There was no healing, the boy suffered and died a horrible death while we all watched.

I stood and faced him. I looked into his blue-gray eyes. I said, Why make it up?

He closed his hands over my arms. His eyes dimmed. Love poured from them. Because the world is full of magic places, he said. I've traveled enough to know. I wanted you to believe one of them was right in your back yard.

We walked down the hill a little way then crossed the ditch and slipped between the barbed wire. We went into the pasture. The only trees were about a hundred yards away, a stand of wilted young elms. They would not provide much shade but they would give a little. I couldn't bear the thought of the baby lying for all eternity under the ruthless sun, in the burning earth. I told Lucas this and he understood. We walked through the waist-high grass hand-in-hand, our feet finding only solid earth—no bogs. We used our hands and fingernails and Lucas's buck knife to scrape out a hole in the hard, dry dirt. We unraveled the black cloth from the baby and laid it down naked in the hole. We crossed ourselves and held our hands over our hearts, we let a moment of silence come and go. Then we pushed the earth back into the hole. The black cloth I held up to the windless sky. The hawk appeared, swooped down, and carried the cloth away in its talons.

Lucas and I stood at the driveway looking out onto the road. He smiled up at the scorching sun.

South, he said, and he looked happy. That's my way. South lies my frontier.

He dug in the pocket of his jeans. He held it up in the sun until it caught the shine. Then he brought it down between us and motioned for me to grasp onto it with him. Our fingertips touched, the coin's golden glow spilling free beneath them. Lucas pressed the coin hard and it snapped cleanly in two halves. He stepped away and pressed his to his heart. His eyes were full and his smile was full. We held a long look at each other. Something passed between us, something was given and given back. Then he slipped the half-coin in his pocket, turned, and strode south. I watched his back vanish over the hill, and when it was gone, I watched it a while longer before starting up the driveway toward the house.

I slipped my half of the coin into my pocket. It pressed cool through the cotton, a momentary relief.

The Cabinet

It was hard to know what it had once held. It was a piece not clearly designed to hold one thing. There were no whitened rings from dinner plates or tea cups, no parallel lines in the dust from book covers on the still varnish-smooth shelves. It might have held curios: miniature ceramic foxes, crystal bells, porcelain dolls with painted faces and stuffed-sock bodies, these wouldn't have left marks. Or maybe my great-grandmother kept it empty for some reason. The panes had been removed and left inch-deep slots in the unfolding doors. The brass hinges were tarnished black and worn silver where they turned. Some of their screws were out and they had to be held in place to open the doors. The wood was still good, though. A hand ran across it without catching splinters, a close look saw a cherry luster under the dust inside the cabinet where over all those years the sun hadn't touched, or rarely. The simple, vine-like carving bordering the drawers showed careful, affectionate work.

Upstairs my father moved about, his steps creaking the ceiling. I stood at the moldy wall and counted seven layers of paper and there must have been more under that. The men were talking in the yard, standing in a line with their backs to the house.

My father's sounds stilled now and then and I wondered what he was doing. I wondered if he was standing in the center of his boyhood room, a room that had been rained in for decades, where wasps had lined the intersections of the slanted walls and ceiling with honeycomb nests and mice had chewed crescents in the rug and strewn ancient, clattering turds, and saying, this was never mine, none of this ever happened.

My father came down with a shovel he must have found upstairs. He let it skip on the battered floor with each step. He held it up like a staff as he went past. We'll save this, he said, and I didn't say anything. He went out the slamming screen door and down the broken walk and poked my brother's back with the shovel and said, Think you can put a new handle on that, blade's like brand new. My brother spiked it in the ground and brought his heel down on the blade's rim, it slid easily into the earth and he nodded. My father came back up the walk, stooping a few times to pull up some sprouts of milkweed worming through the flagstones, even though there were stalks taller than the porch railing round all sides of the house. The men came behind him, heads to the ground.

They took the cabinet in stages. One by one the porcelain-handled drawers in the lower half came out empty and dirt-lined, then the two long, double-handled drawers. They flipped the piece on its flat top and unscrewed the brass clawfeet and one of them looped a length of twine through them and laid them on the windowsill—these wouldn't burn. Four of them closed in on the cabinet's body, hugging it in their eight arms, and eased it carefully through the doorway even though there was no reason to be careful with it. It left a block of unfaded, unnicked wood on the floor. Sun invaded the darker block, covered perhaps half a century, perhaps longer.

They lifted it in the back of the stock trailer with the other pieces: headboards, bookshelves, grayed doors with holes where handles had been, apple and milk crates, rotted planks and a roll of rotted carpeting. They set it on the thin pad of manure that covered the floor of the trailer and the men's boots came out stained damp green. They stood scraping the stinking shreds off their soles using the bumper of the trailer.

My father asked if I was coming and I said I'd walk up the road when I saw the smoke. The men sat on the tailgate kicking each others' legs and joking until my father started the pickup; as they bumped down the drive their hands reached for the edge and gripped it.

I stood on the walk, half-turned to the old house. Pretty soon he would burn it down, too. I didn't want to go back inside and I didn't want to go up the road. I cut behind the house where the clothesline sagged and was draped in cobwebs. As I stood looking at it I heard the faint hum of the pickup motor stop. The air was so still, the overhanging clouds made an insulating dome and I could hear the echoing voices of the men and the trailer gate banging open as they got to work unloading.

The yard was pocked with crabapples. I zigzagged through them, making my way up the slight hill spined with wireless fenceposts that marked the tree strip that had contained my great-grandfather's first cattle, a herd, my family boasted, of about ten. Because now we had nine hundred. A row of horseshoe staples were set in each post for wire to run through, but my father in his thriftiness had long since collected the wire and used it in other fences for much larger pastures. I stopped at a fencepost made of a thick log, its bark hide so unlike the smooth manufactured posts my father bought. I put my hands on its craggy tip and kicked hard at the halfway point until the post split in two, all the fine lengths within crackling the solid quiet as they separated. Good thing we didn't keep cattle in here now.

My grandfather was newly dead. My grandmother had gone six months before him, and now he was the last of my father's ancestors to go, German immigrants who arrived in the middle of Kansas in 1910 and set up homestead on this land. My father worked by his side for fifty years. On that morning, my father waited as was their routine in the idling feed truck for him to hobble out of his pickup and throw back the barbed wire gate to let him pass through in the truck. My father could see the straw hat he wore even in winter on his head through the rear window. It was crushed, the brim broken against the glass because the heart attack had jolted his head back and he should have seen that, gotten to him faster, he thought in hindsight. He found him with his mouth frozen open and lifeless eyes gazing up at the pickup ceiling. Maybe—if he could have gotten to him faster—he should have known something wasn't right. He honked not once, but twice at the already dead father he'd loved so much; now this shamed him though he wouldn't say so. With my father you had to guess at such things, it was the way of the men in these parts.

Now, two weeks after my grandfather's death, when our grief had changed but had not lessened, my father said it was time for a burning, before the summer wind and heat set in and made fires dangerous. He said for years he had been meaning to get rid of the one-room schoolhouse on the hill where my grandmother single-handedly brought him and a handful of neighbor kids up to eighth grade. And while we're at it, we might as well clear the junk, he called it, from the homestead house for kindling. He said I could look, but there was nothing worth saving. Yet he'd found a shovel himself.

There was plenty to burn on my father's thousands of acres of prairie pasture. Mammoth, caved-in barns with more light-bleeding gaps than solid boards in their sides, the chicken houses, crumbling silos and tilted, collapsing homestead houses of my great-grandfather and grandfather's generations, all on land my father now owned. What neighbors remained sometimes saw the smoke and showed up. We sat watching the giant fires from lawn chairs in the road. Once a spark caught dry wheat stubble in the next field and the local fire truck, rusting in a neighbor's barn, had to be revived to put it out. A concrete silo we had to bring down with dynamite, then load the weighty blocks one by one and haul them off to dump in a deep gully with old Model-T car frames and cableless tractors, ancient iceboxes, rusted bedsprings, horses' carcasses. In this way my father kept his pastures clean, at least the high spots and horizons he kept clean.

When I saw the funnel of blue smoke rising in the sky, I descended the ridge and walked in the mud-cracked creek bed to where the bridge crossed the road. I climbed up onto the road and walked down its middle up the long slope of the hill, watching the smoke slowly lengthen out and layer in the blue sky beneath the clouds. Every now and then I saw a flame, a red-orange watery lick in the pale air, flare and then disappear over the hill's arc. Frail white ashes drifted overhead. As I neared I heard the satisfied crackle and hum of the fire chewing and swallowing the wood.

On top of the hill, the prairie stretched out for miles, its bent grasses gray and lavender and yellow. The men stood quieted, watching. My father stood apart from them leaning against a fencepost, his face reddened by the heat or reflection of the fire.

I came alongside him and we stared at it together. It was going good. Everything was going without resistance. I saw the old cabinet, a lovely piece really, that would bring five hundred dollars at the antique store in the town where I went to college, still standing in a shaft of liquid orange, its sides swollen and breathing with heat. The once white walls of the schoolhouse, now streaked with char and warped concave, tremored on the brink of collapse. The little belfry on top had already caved in; I saw the steel bell rocking in the flames on the schoolhouse floor. It would remain among the ashes, and so would the three-foot limestone foundation, blackened but intact.

I asked my father, What about the foundation? What will you do with it?

We'll tear it down with sledgehammers, he said without taking his eyes from the fire. Dynamite if we have to. I want to get rid of everything. I don't want nothing left, he said. I wondered how long that would take, and if it were even possible.

Certain Dawn, Inevitable Dawn

The night we killed my wife neither one of us could sleep. It's because we both feel so guilty, I thought, if we fell easily into a peaceful slumber after our hands had committed such bloody deeds we'd wake feeling even guiltier, we might even begin to question our own humanity because of it, how can I commit murder and not suffer at least one night's insomnia, we'd be thinking in our own heads but terrified to voice it to each other. I must not feel the slightest remorse or guilt or shock, we'd be thinking in the morning light, there must be something wrong with the mechanism of my conscience or, rather, my heart, and if I'm capable of murdering another human being without thinking twice, how can I be capable of really loving one, including this one lying next to me and for whom I've now given up everything? That's how the mind can turn on itself and why killers have to be so careful they don't find themselves falling completely off their rockers and carrying out their own destruction, leaving reckless clues in their wake or rushing to the police to confess like that famous character in literature or even turning the murder weapon on themselves, slitting their own throats or putting the bullet through their own brains. But apparently my mistress's sleeplessness wasn't due to guilt or shock or remorse as mine was (or I wanted to think it was because I couldn't stand the alternative), apparently she really didn't feel any of those feelings so natural to the healthy conscience or human heart but was simply, as she claimed, 'too tired to fall asleep' that night—a phrase I've never understood but there must be some truth to it, enough people use it—she'd had an unusually heavy load of piano lessons at the conservatory and topped off with stabbing my wife to death, it made for a long day.

Neither of us tried to hide our sleeplessness from the other as obliging or overly polite couples do, they lie there back to back, bating their breath and restraining their tosses and turns in an attempt to conceal the fact their eyes are glued open and boring into the darkness as if it were the eternal darkness or original void, when in fact there's nothing eternal about the darkness of a single night and nothing more certain than that that darkness will not last forever—the dawn always comes, even when we don't want it to or aren't ready to see its brutal light. And the darkness in our cheap hotel room was hardly dark, there was a streetlamp right outside the window and its metallic light fell in a gray blade across the bed and our bare bodies half-covered with the over-starched, over-bleached sheets typical of hotel bedding. My mistress and I hadn't blown any money on the room where our post-murder celebration was to take place, she'd insisted (and I agreed) we save our cash for setting up our new household, which was still some distance in the future. We'd have to lay low for a while. I'd have to play the grieving husband and sneak around to see my mistress for a little while longer, we weren't free yet, not yet, for a few more months I'd be taking the back alleys and late-night buses, but instead of behind my wife's back (which now had a six-inch gash in it, though the blood would have stopped flowing from it, it was probably already dry by now) I'd be sneaking around behind the backs of neighbors and policemen and the general population of law-abiding and morally uptight citizens who are always on the lookout for the chance to be a hero and put a killer or deviant behind bars. I'd have to continue to live in my old apartment, too, for some time, I couldn't move in with my mistress right away without arousing suspicion, which was why she had been so careful not to stain the parquet when she drove the dagger between the skinny shoulder blades I knew so well and which my fingers had touched so tenderly so many times— though not lately, not since these other shoulder blades had replaced them—I wouldn't have wanted to see that gruesome reminder every day with my morning coffee. We were willing and prepared to make these minor sacrifices—not much longer, my darling, just a little longer, my love—what we didn't realize was that not only the next few months but the rest of our lives would be spent hiding in the wings and lurking in the shadows. The rest of our lives would be spent ducking the suspicious glance or curious or incriminating question (and all the imagined versions of these), guarding for the slip of the tongue, watching our tracks, wiping our fingerprints and covering our footprints in the snow. There would be no more spotlight for either of us, we'd condemned ourselves to the shadows and we didn't even know it—though I was for the most part already living there, ever since meeting my mistress four or five months ago, we hadn't been together that long but we'd fallen madly in love right off the bat and our passion hadn't declined yet. It would be harder for my mistress to give up the spotlight, she had been a concert pianist for ten years, a few years ago she replaced concerts with lessons but she still gave the occasional faculty recital at her conservatory, now she'd have to give up even that feeble illumination, killers can't afford to draw the slightest attention to themselves, someone in the crowd (one of those uptight moralists or aspiring heroes) might recognize her as the woman they'd brushed past coming out of my apartment building on the night of that terrible—and as yet unsolved!— murder last winter, or five years ago, or ten or twenty . . . But this fact hadn't yet hit home and lying in our shabby hotel room that night, we still thought it was my wife and not ourselves who had made the greater sacrifice. We still thought we had set ourselves free.

My mistress rolled over—we'd been lying back-to-back like those polite couples although unlike them we weren't hiding anything from each other, we both knew the other's eyes were glued wide open—she touched my back, I took her cue and rolled over too. We faced each other in the dimness, the gray blade of the streetlamp fell across her feline face as she propped herself up on one elbow and gazed down at me. My mistress has a very cat-like face, big slanted eyes and a tiny triangular mouth that makes the shape of an anchor when she smiles, her jawbones slope to a menacing point and her brow is broad and high, she's an extraordinary-looking woman. She ran her fingertip along the line of my collarbone and in little circles around my nipple, tender, post-love-making caresses, we'd made love as soon as we got to the hotel (after scrubbing our hands clean of that ill-gotten blood, most of it on my mistress's hands—really the only part I played was to dislodge the knife from the spinal cord so we could throw it in the river later, it had our fingerprints all over it and besides, it was a knife my mistress's mother had given her for carving roasts and would lead the police straight to her door—we went through five or six of those miniature complementary bars of soap, now we'd have to order more from the maid in the morning for our showers, I hoped the unusual order didn't arouse suspicion) and were still, if only vaguely, in the mood. Our love-making wasn't as great as we thought it would be nor did it last very long, we'd anticipated a passionate night of sex but we were both exhausted and feeling guilty—at least I thought we were.

My mistress sighed dramatically. "There were others before you, you know," she said. I could just make out in the dark the upward curl of her delicate lips, the smile like a sailor's tattoo. "Would you like a cigarette?" I said, meaning I would, her comment had caught me off guard. "No, I've quit. From now on I refuse to resemble your wife in any way. Your *former* wife. *Expired* wife." She giggled. My wife was a chain-smoker, she'd have gone to an early grave anyway, a fact which, after (to our credit) much discussion, my mistress and I agreed was certain enough to justify doing her in—at least we were saving her the pain and suffering of a lengthy illness. "I'm quitting too," I said, regretting it already. She: "I'll have to stop wearing earrings, and cut my hair even shorter than it is already—" She flipped her hair over her bare shoulder. There's nothing short about my mistress's stick-straight blue-black hair that falls past her breasts but she has a phobia there is, to her short hair symbolizes getting old and dumpy and that's her greatest fear. "—and I'll have to drop that gesture I fall back on when I'm nervous or feel self-conscious since your wife made a similar gesture, not that there's anything strange about that, many women make it or some version of it, you know, how we touch our hair or face or throat whenever we're about to speak or have just spoken in public or with people who intimidate us, which for most women is virtually everyone— that light, pointless touch to the head or hair or throat, as if we're double-checking our own existence, it's pathetic but you see it in women everywhere." She rolled onto her back and sighed again, this time even more extravagantly. "Where was I? Oh—darling, you must know there were others before you, and I think we're at the point in our relationship where we can tell each other about them without disastrous consequences, don't you?" "Okay," I said. "Do you have any cigarettes?" When I'm nervous I don't fall back on any gestures (that I'm aware of), I smoke or, preferably, chain smoke, a terrible habit I picked up from my wife. She: "You're quitting. You just said so yourself, and I think it's a really good idea. We should both make an effort to forget our former lives completely—that is, *your* former life with *her*—and anything that reminds us of it." "All right, all right. So who were they?"

She closed her eyes as if descending into some inner cave, I suppose she was, the cave of memory, she ran a strand of hair through her lips, tasting it like a little girl, that was one gesture she could do without but I didn't say as much. She said, "I was thinking about him earlier tonight—Eve. For some reason he came to mind just before or as I was killing your wife, you never know what's going to spark old memories." "*Eve?*" "An unusual name for a man, isn't it? At least for someone from our country, which he was not, Eve was from Buenos Aires not that you would know it to look at him or hear him speak, he entered school here when he was ten and so he spoke our language very well, practically without an accent. Also he was fair-haired, dark-eyed and fair-haired, almost flaxen blond, one of his parents must have been European." "Eve," I said reflectively. "The fallen woman, the original sinner who got us all in so much trouble." "I don't know if it's a popular name in Argentina for boys or not, I can't remember ever asking him nor did I ask what his name meant in his language, perhaps I liked the mystery or the sinful connotations his name brought up for me with my rigid Catholic upbringing." That surprised me, my mistress didn't seem the type to have had a rigid Catholic upbringing but now wasn't the time to ask about it, I didn't want to sidetrack her, I was already feeling jealous and I wanted her to get to the reasons why I shouldn't, after all their relationship hadn't lasted. 'At some point it turned sour,' I thought, 'unless it ended because he died, and what are the chances of that'—and yet that's exactly what had happened, though not by accident and not by chance.

" . . . I was crossing the square downtown, it was a beautiful summer night and I'd just given a concert, one of my first big ones. I was still feeling high from it, I've always loved performing whether it goes well or not, but that night in fact went very well, crowds used to leap from their seats after I played, darling, and so they did on that night, I remember I was feeling fabulous as I crossed the square, that devil-may-care mood—along with my famous red skirt—was undoubtedly what attracted Eve to me. And while it's true I was attracted to him, too, the moment I saw him—and I saw him before he saw me—*he* was the one who approached *me* (we were both crossing the square, but Eve was the one who switched directions to come my way)—and darling, you should know I was much more beautiful then than I am now—" It was my turn to give an ironic smile, my obligation as her lover to disagree and I didn't mind doing so, I did find my 'cat-woman' (a name strangers called out at her on the street sometimes, so startling was her resemblance to that animal) very beautiful even if she could look almost sinister in certain light. "—that was fifteen years ago, I was twenty-two and men used to stop dead in their tracks to goggle at me. I wore my skirts shorter, my heels higher, and my hair longer then and men were constantly coming on to me. But I wasn't impressed by the way most of them did it, especially the men—that is, boys—my age, whose pathetic strategy was to let loose catcalls or hoots or whistles while cowering behind their compadres' shoulders. I'd outgrown such adolescent behavior and though I resorted to dating them, I was always on the lookout for what my girlfriends and I called 'a real man.' Eve had already caught my eye— the dark, shadowy eyes, the thick brows and thick lips, the long fair hair pulled back in a ponytail, the broad chest and strong arms under the black leather jacket he wore even though it was a hot night, he was the kind of man who could pick up any woman he wanted and he looked at least thir- ty—definitely 'a real man'—and so my eye caught the mo- ment I caught his and I instantly switched my gaze in the other direction, while he instantly switched his stride in my direction. I looked back and he caught my gaze again, this time he held it and I let him, longer than it was appropri- ate to—that stranger's black-eyed, unblinking and unwaver- ing stare was one of the sexiest moments of my life." *'One of,'* I thought, 'she's carefully qualifying it for my sake and I appreciate it, though I can't help wondering if that mo- ment was *the* sexiest moment of her life and if those she's spent with me don't hold a candle to it, I've never been that bold and women don't want to admit it—especially to them- selves—but nothing turns them on like aggression.'

"There was some sort of festival going on, the square was strung with colorful lights and teenagers were running around shooting off fireworks, as we came face to face a couple of boys ran helter-skelter between us screaming like banshees and shaking sparklers in our faces. Eve scowled and shouted at them to get lost. He turned back to me and flashed a charming smile. 'Excuse me, miss'—he may even have bowed, I think he did—'Where are you going? May I escort you to your rendez-vous?' He held out his arm. It dawned on me I'd been striding quickly and must have looked like I was in a hurry to get somewhere—maybe I was, I may have been late to meet one of my less inspiring lovers and celebrate my concert with him, I can't remember. Nor do I know what made me say what I said next. The fact is I never let strange men pick me up, I didn't take stupid risks like that, not in this city known for its rapists and murderers and mafiosi (back then it was even more dangerous—that's when that serial killer was on the loose, the one who sewed up the body parts of his victims inside stuffed animals, do you remember that weirdo?). No doubt it's as simple as the fact that Eve turned me on that I said what I said, which was some version of: 'Oh, I'm not meeting anyone, I'm not doing anything, I don't have anywhere to go.' Instantly I regretted it, I sounded far too eager and too available, no doubt I was touching my throat or face or hair like a madwoman. Eve's thick brows shot up and he shrugged. 'A woman as beautiful as you? My luck is looking up.' He was still holding out his arm. I took it.

"We had a glass of wine—he paid—sitting outdoors at that little place, it's still there, next to the big sportswear store (though I don't think the store was there then) and the fountain with the giant leaping fish, if you sit at the corner table you get sprayed by its mouth?" I knew the place, my wife and I had gone there often in our early days and we'd even gotten wet at that corner table. "He told me about his boyhood in Buenos Aires—mountains over the sea, pythons and red wine, slaving away on the sugar cane farm and so on, such clichéd South American remembrances it might at least have *occurred* to me he was making them up (I still don't know if he was), it didn't, my naïve eyes and ears were too busy seeing and hearing what they wanted to, that is, the shine in his eyes and the longing in his voice when he spoke of his homeland, how sweet, I thought, the little jungle boy far away from home—nothing, darling, turns a woman on like seeing the little boy in the man.

"We walked around the square, strolling leisurely, I was holding his arm as if I was his wife, then Eve turned onto a dark street. You know how as soon as you turn onto one of those side streets off the square it's suddenly pitch black not to mention run-down, suddenly it feels like you're in the ghetto or underbelly of the city, I don't know why they don't put more streetlamps on those streets or keep up the ones that are there, so many tourists go down them and it's a well-known fact most of our robberies, rapes, and murders take place there (but not all of them, as we well know, ha ha), it's like that now and it was even worse then. We passed by some iron gates and a dog leapt at us from the shadows, barking and baring its fangs. I was starting to feel a little nervous. I looked at Eve, his face was hidden in the same shadows but he must have been able to see my face all right because he leaned down and brought his lips close to my ear. 'Hey,' he whispered. 'You want to go somewhere? I want you to meet some friends of mine.' Even if he is a creep, I thought, I'll be safe with other people around, it might even turn out to be one of those wild, unforgettable party nights I'll look back on with envy in my old age . . .

"We went back to the square and hopped in a cab. It was a long, convoluted ride with many backtracks and wrong turns and screeching stops. Eve kept popping up like a jack-in-the-box between the bucket seats to bark directions in the cabbie's ear: 'Stop! Stop! Wrong way!' or, at the last minute, 'Here, the turn is here!', or exasperated, as if he couldn't believe our luck getting the stupidest driver in the world, 'Back up, back up, back up, we missed it again.' The cab wound down rickety cobblestone alleys and up steep, nearly vertical inclines, such streets as I'd had no idea inhabited this city I grew up in. Eve even went to the point of encouraging the cabbie to drive dangerously ('Run it, run it, we can make it!'). What was worse is the cabbie was up for it, he grinned and put his leadfoot down, plowing the car through red lights and around hairpin curves, the cabbie was getting some thrills in his typically boring night and at the same time getting to show off his daredevil driving skills. In the middle of all this Eve found time to put his hand on my bare knee, I was wearing a very short red skirt and no stockings (of course I changed after my concerts, at which I wore magnificent strapless sequined ballgowns), I remember exactly the one, in fact I still have that skirt, it's hanging in my closet at home though I haven't worn it in years. It has a seam stitched in silver thread on the ass the shape of a lightning bolt, it's really racy, I could never get away with wearing it now, my legs aren't what they used to be if my hips haven't changed that much. Eve put his hand on my knee but he didn't move it up or down or give little squeezes or light caresses with his fingertips, none of that, it was like he glued his hand to my leg and forgot about it. Even as he sprang up and down like an amphetamined jack-in-the-box, yelling at the cabbie, sinking back on the seat, his hand didn't budge. Keep in mind this was the first time he had touched me, I mean, in a provocative or intimate way, and here he was taking it totally for granted." 'The ungrateful touch,' I thought, 'is worse than no touch at all.' My mistress and I weren't touching ourselves at the moment, we'd never been one of those couples who have to touch all the time. Now we were both lying on our backs gazing into the ratty blanket of darkness overhead, it never gets completely dark in a city this size and the eyes never get a break from the exhausting duty or overwhelming obligation or boring chore of seeing. "This selfish streak or blind egotism or machismo in Eve is what eventually made me do what I did that night, I mean he brought it on himself, at the same time all the signs were there in the beginning and I should have seen them—'the end is in the beginning,' whoever said that." My mistress liked to quote lofty or literary sayings as well as folksy proverbs, in fact I didn't think she could tell the two apart. "He only remembered to unglue his hand (it was like he'd forgotten it was part of his body, his and not mine) when at last we pulled up in front of the castle—that's what I call it in my memory and it really was an impressive building. Its windowless stone facade towered several stories above the bourgeois apartment buildings hugging it on either side—oddly enough, it was sitting right in the middle of a rather typical middle-class residential area. Only the turrets rising out of its steep bronze rooftops showed any windows and these were mere slivers embedded in the stone, the castle looked like a medieval fortress braced for attack, perhaps that part of town was more dangerous than it looked. I immediately forgave Eve his dead fish hand, I'd never gone out with a rich man and it looked like I was getting my chance. After exchanging some chummy chuckles with the reckless cabbie and tipping him extravagantly, while at the same time, whether he intended it or not, conjuring or re-conjuring himself in my eyes as a sophisticated man of the world, Eve extended his elbow and I looped my arm in it (he was acting like a gentleman again), it was a gesture that was becoming ours. As he escorted me up the broad stone steps, the massive blocks of the façade glowed silver in the moonlight or rather, streetlight, but to my Cinderellaed eyes—ha ha, I don't think I've ever used that as a verb"—'and you're not now,' I thought, 'that's an adjective you've just used,' but I didn't point it out, I was madly in love with my mistress and her little flaws didn't bother me that much, I put on my own rose-colored glasses—"that steely aura could only be moonlight. The front steps forked in two branches and curled around a dried-up fountain set in an overgrown tangle of bristling, blackish plants. On a closer look, I was startled to see those plants were ladyfingers, one of the most poisonous plants on the planet. In high school, darling, I was obsessed with two things: piano and dangerous plants. Don't ask me how the two fit together, I only remember it was the Venus flytrap with its malicious, consciously snapping jaws, a plant that catches every kid's imagination, that got me started, only I took it further than everybody else and went on to study on my own poison-needled cacti, scarlet fever wild roses, the python vines of the Amazon, so often mistaken for actual snakes by their victims, and indeed—but I never imagined I'd see them in person—those almost extinct and exquisitely beautiful ladyfingers, so named for their long, fuzzy, tapered leaves that look like they're covered in black velvet, they resemble old-fashioned ladies' evening gloves but their edges are sharp as daggers, a mere brush can open the skin and infuse a deadly venom. I gasped as I saw they filled not only the entire central garden, but trailed around

both sides of the castle in dense rows, they must have encir-
cled the whole building—a vicious, living moat. I was trembling, but Eve didn't seem inclined to push me into them
as he escorted me up the steps, at the same time he didn't
caution me to keep my bare calves clear of them, he didn't
remark on the black bushes at all and I had to wonder if he
knew what they were—and, too, what sort of 'friends' we
were coming to visit . . .

"At the high double doors Eve punched in a complicated
code. A voice came on the intercom, I couldn't understand
it for the pounding rock-n-roll music in the background, but
Eve spoke back and the bolts clicked open. No cross-eyed
butler or crotchety maid appeared to greet us, in fact, we
stepped into a pitch black hall, Eve had to fumble around at
the wall to find the lights but it didn't take him long, he'd
obviously been here a hundred times (he must have usually
taken a limousine whose driver knew where the castle was,
I thought). Eve was impatiently tugging at my hand but I
insisted on having a look around, it turned out just as he
said, a big letdown. While the building truly was a castle and
quite impressive architecturally, probably built in the 1800s
by some prince or sheikh or baron or mogul, the grand-
sons or great-grandsons he'd passed it down to—and whom
I was about to meet at the height of their glory—hadn't
treated it so well. The ceiling of the central hall rose up
like a Gothic cathedral's and the marble railings of the up-
per three stories lined the interior, but the walls and floors,
which should have been draped with tapestries and Persian
rugs and hung with magnificent paintings, were bare and all
the rooms deserted even of furniture. The only signs of life
we found in the library—its twenty-feet high shelves were
bare, but scotch-taped to the mahogany paneling were three
faded posters of Tom Cruise in *Mission Impossible I, II,* and
III (in that order) and a few crinkled beer cans (of the cheap-
est brand) rolled around on the barren floor.

"Eve led me into the guts of the castle, through the kitchen
(stacks of moldy dishes and a few crusts of bread—so someone did live here) and the long narrow corridors back of it,

at last we reached a thick wooden door, it wasn't locked, we ducked into a dark cobbled stairway such as hump-backed dungeon wardens tread down, lanterns hoisted before them. Down, down, down we went for a long time, like miners into the earth, at last I heard the faint sounds of music—well, I wouldn't really call it music, it was the same outdated, throbbing American rock-n-roll we'd heard on the intercom. Through another wooden door we came onto the party: thirty or forty people, barely-dressed women writhing (that is, attempting to belly dance but their moves were really rough, probably because they were drunk and high and not because they lacked talent or rhythm) at the far end of the room, greasy men playing cards or lounging on couches and guzzling that cheap brand of beer from huge cans, the lights, oddly, turned up bright, and a viscous umbrella of cigarette and hashish smoke hovering over it all. The room was furnished exactly like a modern suburban basement, had it formerly been a dungeon they must have spent a lot of time if not money remodeling it, not a trace of castle remained. The décor was early seventies—black shag carpeting, faux pine paneling, a few ratty orange couches and an enormous, badly ripped leather one with the stuffing oozing out like a mass of white worms. A couple of metal card tables and a crooked pool table (not in use)—and I'd been expecting black silk suits, martinis, pearls and champagne . . .

"Eve led me to the big leather couch and we squeezed onto it, instantly a pack of mongrels crowded around us, or rather, me, leering and grinning, their legs opening and their hands closing together, gold-toothed guys with over-greased black curls and high-dollar leather jackets exactly like Eve's. They were obviously foreigners but I couldn't pin down from what country, they didn't look South American, and like Eve they were speaking our language fluently and with little or no accent. They were also obviously in the drug trade, their elongated pinky fingernails were sharpened to razor points like woodblock carving tools—not unlike the leaves of those guardians of their fortress—but these weapons had their own deadly designs, even I knew they were for cutting cocaine, opium, heroine—if not windpipes. I tried to pick out the ringleader but it's hard to tell who's in charge when people are partying, then even the evil ringleader is everybody's buddy, he's generous with his compliments and slaps on the back and drops sentimental comments such as 'we're all family here, we're all brothers,' he'd run his fingernail through your windpipe in a heartbeat if he felt so inclined and everyone knows it. But they were all dropping sentimental phrases like that and they all seemed to be trying to flatter each other, probably eager to get in each others' good graces while they were drinking it up and avert a bullet in the back or a throat-slit in bed later on in the night. The giant hookah was making the rounds (the whole scene was depressing, it reminded me of high school, or high school with black market criminals). Suddenly someone tipped it over, that's when the ringleader revealed himself. It was the short wiry guy—it's always the runt, he's got the biggest chip on his shoulder—with tiny gold hoop earrings and a scar like a horizon line running the width of his forehead. He'd just started telling stories about his homeland, he was waxing nostalgic, drifting back (hashish makes you sentimental), when the hookah toppled. Eve and the others rushed to save it, cursing and forgetting all about the runt's reminiscences. The runt didn't even stand up, he just gave a single atomic bark—like a bullet issuing from his diminutive body—'SIT!'—and the whole room hushed, the immediate group folded back onto their couches like puppets, leaving the toppled hookah on the carpet. The head honcho picked up where he'd left off, he was remembering the golden days of his boyhood when he and his brothers (some of which had to be in the room, his blood brothers as well as drug brothers, the men all looked exactly alike—Eve with his blond ponytail was the only misfit) used to kill the neighbors' chickens for sport by hanging them from carefully constructed chicken-size gallows they built themselves from debris they gathered from the streets, those were the days . . . But they always tortured them a while before killing them—Eve asked how, precisely, he wanted the details, it was a little boy's question but in this case I didn't find it particularly charming—or maybe he was just trying to get back into the good graces of his touchy host, who was only too glad to tell him how they whittled sticks razor-sharp and poked them through the dangling, squawking chickens' bodies at various points, like demon biologists they'd study the various hues and textures of goo retrieved on the sticks and speculate on which organ it came from and what disease it was certainly carrying, it was a real scientific enterprise. They were in the process of building a guillotine to go with the gallows when the family moved, leaving behind their torture contraptions for the next family to wonder at—or use, who knows, maybe that next family was as perverted as theirs . . . " My mistress paused. "Recalling this conversation, darling, makes me recall another one I had only recently, really it wasn't a conversation but a monologue or something I heard a stranger say the other day on the bus, I had never heard such a thing at that time, that night with Eve, but if I had I would have been thinking of it and might even have repeated the words (and tried to pass them off as my own) as a way of entering the conversation or attempting to impress or, perhaps, offend Eve and the ringleader." "I didn't know you rode the bus," I said. "Don't you usually take a cab?" My mistress shrugged. "I usually do, but it was raining hard the other day after my piano lessons and I didn't feel like standing out on the curb so I hopped on the bus. It turned out to be a much longer ride than I'd anticipated—" 'That's right,' I thought, 'the buses in this city suck beans.' "—the route wound all over the city with no apparent rhyme or reason. Anyway, to get back to my anecdote—at one point it stopped in a bad neighborhood. A middle-aged woman wearing a nice suit and a modest string of pearls was sitting next to me and we stared out the window together, looking for some entertaining sight to pass the time as you do on the bus. A group of boys was standing on the dirt curbside in the rain, they were holding big long sticks, sharp sticks—perhaps branches they'd carved and polished though I don't know where they would've gotten branches in that ghetto, there's not a tree for miles around, more likely they'd made them from debris they found in the streets, in any case they were holding them up like spears, one boy, the fat one, pointed his like a gun at the clouds and mocked shooting them, the others slapped the ground or whacked the telephone pole, they were bursting with aggression, itching for something to strike, wound, or, even better, kill—that's when the woman next to me said, she may simply have been talking to herself or thinking aloud without realizing it, I don't think her eyes ever did meet mine: 'Little boys are champions of death. They love shooting, killing, dismembering . . . it looks brutal, it looks terrible from outside, but what they're really doing is seeking the infinite, the eternal pattern or timeless presence beyond death is what violent little boys are really after. They don't know it, of course, they think they're just having fun, but in the blood and gore of their animal or insect or, in the worst case, human victims, they're really treasure-hunting, and if they don't find the gold or are never given the chance to seek it—say their violent instincts are reined in by uptight parents or repressed society, they become the boys who grow up to be criminals. They become our gang thugs, rapists, psychopaths, hired and serial killers—even our soldiers and policemen—without even knowing it, they choose worlds where violence is the currency of choice so the desire they're driven by—to peek behind the mask of death—can have full rein.' She must have been a psychologist or scholar, she obviously knew what she was talking about (whether her theories are correct or not) and she spoke like a true intellectual. Had that conversation already happened then, I may have been more forgiving of the fact that Eve was completely ignoring me for a description of what chickens' feet look like when you scrape the yellow ribbing off with your pocketknife (stringy, cellular, ringed like the inner rings of a tree), as it was it really pissed me off—here I am, I thought, looking better than I ever will again in my miniature skirt and long long hair long as only young girls can wear it, and I won't be young that much longer"—'it's still the same,' I thought, 'your hair is still that long and you're still that beautiful,' what I really meant or wanted to believe was 'you look as good for me as you did for him, he didn't get anything I'm not getting'—"and my date, or rather, my pick-up, is treating me like dirt. Now Eve wasn't even touching me with his dead fish hand, nor his knee or even his gaze, his gaze bounced between the ring-leader's animated face and the giant smoking hookah and his legs were spread wide in anticipation of its arrival as it made the rounds. Which was why, no doubt, he didn't notice the pack of men goggling me—pretty soon they were inching, creeping, and sidling their way closer, closer, closer to my apparently magnetic body. One was particularly driven, the most repulsive one, of course, and no doubt the most sex-deprived, a craggy-faced hunchback who had managed to squeeze in beside me, now he was stretching his curled yellow wart-spotted fingers out to touch my bare knee (the other one, maybe he thought this one was fair game, it didn't bear Eve's leaden handprint). I knocked the hand away, he giggled and the hand dipped inside his leather jacket and came back, only this time it was gripping a knife. It pressed the cold blade into the flesh beneath my ribs, I screamed but no one paid any attention, perhaps the rock-n-roll was so loud no one heard, or perhaps they simply didn't care . . .

"The hunchback set to licking my neck like a cow. I reached for Eve but one of the belly dancers, the one with long plastic curly eyelashes and a giant eighties hairdo it looked like she'd done on those old-fashioned hot rollers had squeezed between us. Not that she was picking up on Eve, she was too out of her mind to make any moves like that—her head lolled back on the couch and her legs fell as wide open as Eve's, I had the urge to close them but my captor was holding me tight by the elbow and he wasn't letting up on the knife. I didn't know whether she had any underwear on or not—" "'Underwear?'" I said. "Don't you call them 'panties'?" "No." My mistress shook her head definitively. "That's a male fantasy. Men say 'panties,' women don't. Women use the more down-to-earth term since that piece of clothing isn't nearly as interesting to them as it is to men. Anyway, she didn't look the type to wear underwear and she was too out of it to notice that the guys on the opposite couch could see up inside her or maybe that's what she wanted, maybe she wanted masculine eyes to crawl up inside her like a miner's lamp, if so she'd have to get their attention, at the moment they were too out of it themselves to notice that chance so coveted among men. At last I was able to reach behind the belly dancer's shoulders and tug on Eve's jacket sleeve, he paid no attention, even when I punched him on the neck. When he finally did look my way it was because his host pointed out something in that direction, a belly dancer was contemplating taking her top off. Eve had the stupidest grin on his face, he was in another world and I could see he was in no shape to be my hero even if he'd felt inclined to. The hunchback was uncoiling his tongue in my ear, his stubby penis poking up in his pants, he was really getting turned on and his distraction was causing his grip on the knife to slip—I felt my chance. I jumped up and ran stumbling (the hookah had landed in my hands a few times too) through the door we'd come in, slamming it behind me.

"Pitch darkness closed in. The little lamps affixed to the walls that had feebly lit our way down were now out, either they'd all burned out at once or someone had turned them out. That's when the chilling thought first occurred to me that there was something funny going on in that basement, something not quite right about that party scene, a dark understanding hovered at the edge of my vision, suddenly I was swept into a horror movie fantasy (hashish makes you imaginative as well as sentimental), I saw bloody knives, mangled bodies, *Basement Bloodbath* came to mind as a possible title. I started climbing frantically in the dark, clawing at the craggy walls and uneven steps, sometimes on all fours. The only way I could get lost, I knew, was to slip into one of those side passageways I'd glimpsed as I followed Eve down, my finger looped in the belt strap of his leather jacket as if we'd been lovers for years—that's how it was with us, I don't know, kind of like it was when we met, darling, so familiar and so easy, as if we'd been together in a past life or something. Up, up, up the twisting stairs I climbed, who knows how long, it's easy or inevitable to lose track of time in the dark (while in the light we're enslaved by and obsessed with it and with making every second count), still I didn't come to a door, only more twists and turns. Finally I began to think—then, to *know* I'd slipped off course, in spite of my warning to myself I must have slipped into one of those side passageways and gotten lost in the guts of the castle. At any moment, I thought, I'll run across a skeleton, I'll hear my feet rattling bones and reach down to grasp a skull, that's what always happens in those horror flicks, that or she hears footsteps in the distance, yes, there they are, footsteps approaching, approaching, clack clack clack clack, echoing, echoing—the gleam of the hunchback's knife rose in my mind, he was coming to seek his vengeance for my rejection—clack clack scuffle clack scuffle . . . it sounded like the pilot of those undoubtedly masculine feet (they were too heavy to be a woman's and besides they weren't high heels, back then no woman would be caught dead on the town in flats, now we're more comfortable and our posture better but we're not as sexy) was drunk or high or both, the steps were clumsy and erratic rather than determined and inevitable as they are in the movies. I cried out: 'Eve! Eve! Is that you coming?' But—just as in those flicks—no one answered. Whoever he was he had to hear my cries, the steps were getting louder and louder and closer and closer. So I did what the petrified heroine in the horror flicks does, she stands there shaking in her boots (I mean her heels) and it drives you mad, you want to reach into the television or movie screen and shake her, thrust her into motion but, of course, you can't, so you grit your teeth and clench your fists, you writhe in your seat and your feet twitch with the instinct to run, you can't stand it any longer, not one second longer, at that moment—"

Suddenly my mistress raised up and looked out the window. I could see her triangular feline face and the sharp points of her dagger eyelashes clearly in the whitening light, the dawn was approaching, the certain dawn, inevitable dawn. "Shahrazade stops here," she said softly, almost as if to herself. "And saves her life." "On the first 999 nights," I said. "On the thousandth she finishes her story—in the broad daylight—but it doesn't matter, by now the king has fallen hopelessly in love with her and can't possibly bring himself to chop her into pieces as he'd promised." I really didn't know if that's how that antiquated and monstrously long tale ended, I'd never made it past the twenty or thirtieth night and I was counting on it my mistress hadn't either, she can play the piano but she knows almost nothing about literature. "Go on, go on."

She took a deep breath, as if gathering steam for her finale. "Well, it happened just like it happens early on in those horror movies, in those teasing but all the same terrifying scenes well before the climax, when it turns out to be not the killer but the girlfriend or graveyard keeper or janitor or boyfriend—it was Eve shuffling up those steps, and when he had come so close I could feel his hot breath (though I still didn't know it was his), he grabbed my arms and clamped them to my sides, he mashed his lips onto mine, apparently he could see better in the dark than I could because he wasn't far off the mark. I wasn't that familiar with Eve's smell and every one of those mongrels including the warty hunchback had had on a leather jacket, and so for the duration of that brutal, never-ending kiss in the total darkness, I didn't know who I was kissing or if the knife that had already left its mark had returned to open my flesh this time, I didn't know until I started getting into it—I'm not ashamed to say I was really getting turned on, passion and terror are two sides of the same coin—" 'My god,' I thought, 'it's true, women really do secretly love the feeling of being overpowered, that's not to say they want to be raped or that men should have the right to rape them, that's taking it too far, but once it's happening they usually enjoy it, though they'd never admit it.' "—finally I reached my arms around his neck and felt Eve's ponytail. It's too bad he couldn't have stopped there, had he I may have fallen in love with him. But he didn't—Eve hadn't invested all that time buying me wine and dragging me around on his elbow for nothing . . . he went ahead and took what he wanted—that is, I mean, darling, he raped me." She stopped, it was my turn to say something. I did: "Oh. Well." I didn't dare say what I was thinking, which was, 'You didn't want to?' I pushed that thought aside, knowing how dangerous it was, and instead I started thinking about the butt in my jacket pocket. 'I'm sure there's one in there,' I thought. 'That one I didn't toss

on our way here because we were walking by the fancy ho-
tels with their snobby doormen, there might be some tobacco left in it, but now is not the time to get up and get it.'
I did anyway, I found it and slipped back in bed and lit it,
there wasn't much there but filter. My mistress didn't say
anything, she was so engrossed in her painful memories she
didn't notice or perhaps she really didn't care whether I quit
smoking or not, despite what she said. "Well," I said again.
"I'm sorry." "There's more," she said. "Go on."

"Eve was in an incredibly foul mood on the way back up. He
kept dropping his cigarette lighter (which he was using to
see by) and cursing the darkness. 'I've always hated these
fucking lanterns, they turn off automatically if no one's on
the stairs for a while and no one will tell me the code to
turn them back on, it makes no sense . . . ' but the moment
we emerged from the stairwell his asshole or rapist switch
flipped off and his gentleman switch flipped on, he held
out his arm and flashed his charming smile—like an actor
bewitched by some devil director, he seemed to have no
control over which part he was playing. I almost felt sorry
for him. Out on the front steps I saw the black-gloved ladyfingers glistening in the streetlamp light. I bent to look at
them. 'What beauties!' I cried. 'If only I had one of them in
my bedroom windowsill or on my balcony railing, if only a
cutting . . . oh, so gorgeous . . .' I really piled it on. Just as
women can't resist the little boy in the man, men can't resist
the little girl in the woman, the girl who fusses over flower
petals and pretty ribbons, sure enough Eve's masculine instincts kicked in and he bent to the ladyfingers. His hands
seized the sharp, poisonous leaves, apparently sex hadn't
sobered him up and he was still so wasted he didn't feel the
cuts or the burn, he went at a giant stem, tugging and bend-
ing and eventually twisting it fiercely, it wouldn't break, the
plant didn't want to give up its own, it kept twisting and
twisting and twisting, it was maddening, even I was becoming annoyed at its stubbornness. Finally Eve sank his teeth
into the vulnerable spot, he was so engrossed in this chival-
rous project it was no trouble at all to tip him off the steps
with my high heel in his ass. He tumbled into the shrubs,

to top it off his head cracked on the fountain, that was a bonus. I ran off down the street, now he'd have to listen to the click click click of my heels fading in the distance as I'd had to listen to the clack clack clack (or rather, clack clack scuffle clack scuffle) of his approaching. The last memory I have of Eve is him hunched over in that poisonous patch of black velvet, holding his head and screaming after me, 'Demon bitch! Demon bitch!' Ha ha, that nickname always makes me laugh, at least it's creative, it must have been the hashish that came up with it."

My mistress laid her head on my chest. "Eve," she sighed. "I really liked him. What a strange, romantic night. But he shouldn't have treated me so badly . . . " I dragged frantically on the soggy butt. "The thing was, every one in a thousand people are immune to ladyfingers' venom, and so I couldn't be sure I'd gotten him, I was forced to scan the obituaries for the next several days, there are so many papers in this city and not knowing his last name made it that much harder. And you know, darling, it's so weird but as I was doing that scanning, as my eye roved over all those fading, expired names, the feeling came over me that that roving and scanning eye was *causing* his name to appear there, as I sat on the floor of my apartment with the papers spread over my piano bench, with each page I flipped and each gaze I drilled between the lines of the names of those unknown dead, I couldn't shake the feeling it was not the poisonous plants or the crack on the head that was killing, would kill, or had already killed Eve—no, the killer was my own laser eye which *would not stop* looking until it saw what it absolutely had to see, that singular, unusual name, *Eve, Eve*, name of the original sinner, *Eve, Eve, Eve,* day and night the obsessed eye chanted the name—until, at last, it did see it."

She shuddered. "It was eerie. I can't explain the feeling. And it didn't go away when I finally knew he was dead—the description of his death confirmed that that Eve was my Eve— in fact my paranoia intensified, my mind turned on me and I became so terrified the police were going to knock on my door that I roamed the streets for days, sleeping on friends' floors or in the baby grands at school. But the police never did show up. Let's hope they don't this time either."

No sooner had the words left her mouth than a knock sounded on the door. Or rather, a rap—hard, demanding. Not the kind of knock the maid gives, not at five in the morning. We looked at each other, frozen, wide-eyed. "They must have found her," I whispered. We hadn't counted on that, I was supposed to discover the body late the following afternoon upon arriving home from my 'business trip.' I jumped out of bed and fumbled for my boxer shorts and pants. "You're putting on your pants?" my mistress hissed. "Don't you think we should get out of here first?" "What, naked? We'll attract even more attention running down the street naked!" The knock came again. Louder, angrier. She rushed to the window, dragging the sheet. "We have to jump." "Are you crazy? It's six stories down, we'll kill ourselves." No doubt having heard the frantic activity behind the door, the knocker began to pound even more furiously. A man's voice shouted: "Veronika! Veronika, I know you're in there and I know who you're with! Open the door, you bitch, there's no getting off this time!" I waited for my mistress to turn around, she was standing at the window with her back to me. She turned in slow motion, like a life-size doll or a mannequin revolving in a window display. "That's not a name," I whispered evenly, my eyes leveled at her, "you sometimes go by, is it?" The anchor appeared in her little lips. "No, darling," she said. "I've never liked that name." I buttoned my pants and opened the door, wide enough so he could see my mistress was not his wife or, more likely, mistress—I doubted he would have been chasing so ardently after his wife. He was bare-chested himself and gripping a hammer in his hand. A stranger driven by his own dark desires, who knew nothing about ours and wouldn't have given a damn if he had, he wasn't one of those prudish moralists we'd have to look out for from now on. "Try next door," I said. He looked sheepish and went away down the hall, not trying any of the other doors. "It's a good thing he had the wrong door," my mistress said. "He was about to kill someone."

My mistress was back in bed. I lay down beside her and retrieved the mangled butt from the bedside ashtray, all the
tobacco was long gone but I sucked on it anyway, I was feeling a little nervous. Finally, I asked what I'd been putting
off asking: "So, demon bitch, ha ha,"—I was trying to sound
light-hearted—"is there anyone else you've murdered you
want to tell me about?" "Ha ha yourself," she said. "It's not
the kind of thing I do every day, though I can't speak for
my evil eye." 'What's that supposed to mean,' I thought
but didn't dare voice it, nor did she bother to clarify. She
went on: "Violence is not a fascination for women as it is
for men, darling—an obsession, an outward desire. For
women violence is a natural and necessary state of being
crucial to survival, though very few of us ever learn to act
on it." She rolled onto her belly and burrowed into my body,
the sun fell across her bare shoulder blades and her black
hair gleamed like sheet metal. The light was getting in my
eyes and the traffic noises beginning below, the dawn had
passed, the day had come. My mistress sighed. "Go to sleep,
darling. The thousandth night is over," she whispered. She
tightened her arms around me. "And we're finally free."

About the Author

Tasha Haas's fiction and poetry have appeared in *Conjunctions, Coal City Review, Flint Hills Review, South Dakota Review, Stickman Review,* and elsewhere. She teaches creative writing, children's literature, and composition at Kansas City Kansas Community College. She earned her M.F.A. in Fiction Writing from Bowling Green State University. She is the winner of the Langston Hughes Award for Fiction, and has earned competitive writing and teaching residencies in Costa Rica and Lithuania. Tasha grew up on a ranch on the prairie flatlands of southwestern Kansas, the land and culture of which has been a strong influence in her writing. Her extensive travels in Europe, Eastern Europe, Russia, and Latin America have also given her many stories. This is her first book.

www.ingramcontent.com/pod-product-compliance
Lightning Source LLC
Chambersburg PA
CBHW051851170626
46807CB00003B/1424